CRACKING
the CODE

AYUSHMANN KHURRANA is an award-winning Indian film actor, singer and television anchor whose debut film, *Vicky Donor*, was critically acclaimed and a huge commercial success.

TAHIRA KASHYAP is a professor of mass communication and journalism in Mumbai and the author of two books. She also writes and directs plays in Chandigarh, her hometown.

CRACKING
the CODE

Ayushmann Khurrana
and Tahira Kashyap

RUPA

Published by
Rupa Publications India Pvt. Ltd 2015
7/16, Ansari Road, Daryaganj
New Delhi 110002

Sales Centres:
Prayagraj Bengaluru Chennai
Hyderabad Jaipur Kathmandu
Kolkata Mumbai

Copyright © Ayushmann Khurrana and Tahira Kashyap 2015

The views and opinions expressed in this book are the
authors' own and the facts are as reported by him
which have been verified to the extent possible, and
the publishers are not in any way liable for the same.

All rights reserved.
No part of this publication may be reproduced, transmitted,
or stored in a retrieval system, in any form or by any means,
electronic, mechanical, photocopying, recording or otherwise,
without the prior permission of the publisher.

ISBN: 978-81-291-3568-1

Fifth impression 2023

10 9 8 7 6 5

Printed in India

This book is sold subject to the condition that it shall not, by way of
trade or otherwise, be lent, resold, hired out, or otherwise circulated,
without the publisher's prior consent, in any form of binding or
cover other than that in which it is published.

I dedicate this book to all those fans/strugglers/aspirants who have just boarded their trains or flights to come to this city of dreams—ones who dwell on the kutcha roads of Aaram Nagar; who give out their profiles while holding a placard in front of them day in and day out. I also dedicate it to those strugglers who have given up and gone back, only to return. You inspired me to write this one.

Contents

Prologue

DO YOU WANT to be rich? Do you want to be famous? Do you want to be successful? If the answer is yes, then quit reading the book right away. But if you are lazy, easily bored or have some time to kill, read on...

I want to begin this book with utmost honesty. And let me assure you that this isn't an attempt to be pompous, vain or preachy. I have read quite a few books written by legends and can safely say that this is perhaps the most 'un-legendary' (that's not even a word, by the way) stuff to be published so far. All I can assure you is that there is nothing in here that is going to be pretentious.

Considering the fact that you have read this far, let me just say that wealth, fame and success are qualities that are relative. For some, being the top industrialist is all about being rich; for others, making it to Forbes' Most Powerful list is the ultimate degree of being successful; while for someone else, having the best confectionary shop (for example) in their own small city is the definition of success.

But what is that one secret longing that unites you and me? What is that fantasy we all (or at least most of the readers who have picked up this book) have nurtured? It's the love of the stage. The love of Bollywood. It's about being an actor, wanting to become an actor, choosing your own acting niche, aspiring for the stage. It's about being in awe of the lights, the camera and the action, wanting to be labelled as a 'nautanki', to be called a 'dramebaaz', yearning for people to acknowledge the hero or the heroine in you, and no matter how derogatory it sounds, but liking it when someone refers to you as an 'actor saala'.

And this is precisely what I was born to be. This is what I am today. This is what I want to share with you and this is what I see in the people who have, time and again, reached out to me through SMS, Whatsapp, email, Facebook, Twitter or through snail mail; some of you even stalked me for it. This is my way of saying thank you to 'the one' who helped me tread the path to being an actor; the path that has some rules to it, the journey that has a definite pattern, the destiny that awaits those who recognize these codes.

Again, it's a personal opinion. For those seeking nirvana, what I'm saying could be nonsensical or trashy 'gyaan'. But for the 'mango people', I hope this makes sense. So my question here is, how badly do you want be an actor? Do you have it in you to become one? Did you always want to be on stage? Do you dream of looking at your movie's poster being splashed around the city? Do you want to be the one who is chased for autographs and photographs? Do you want to be nominated and awarded for your acting prowess? Looking at others, do you get troubled by thoughts like 'why not me' or 'wish I was there'? Or you mutter to yourself: 'Isse accha toh main hi kar lun, bas chance hi nahi mila', or even 'Ayushmann, saala lucky bastard!'

Sure thing, but then how did this 'lucky bastard' became the talk of the town? Was it luck, karma, or was there a code? I'm not trying to sound pompous here, but as I sit back to reminisce upon the story of my journey so far, I think I recognize a pattern. A code of sorts, that applied to me at a sub-conscious level. 'It' applying at a sub-conscious level could be termed as either karma or luck. But 'its' existence is certainly not by chance. It's definitely out there. We just need to reach out for it. And, hopefully, after reading this book, your approach to 'it' would be at a more conscious level. It may sound abstract or even frivolous at this moment, but then there are still many of us who find Maslow's laws a waste of time, Einstein's theories a fluke and Shakespearean plays a result of a whimsical mind.

I am not saying that this book has foolproof formulas to becoming successful. But these are palpable codes that will make you receptive to success the way these cryptographic signals helped me attain the however modest position I am at today. These codes are no rocket science. This is just my story so far.

So, I ask you simply, chance chahiye kya? If the answer is yes, then this is the book to read. Of course, I can't assure you that you'll become the next Amitabh Bachchan or Shah Rukh Khan after reading this book. This is my humble attempt to share my journey, my anecdotes, my experiences, my codes that have helped me become an actor. Success, wealth and fame, like I said before, are relative. Many of you reading this might consider my attempt too ambitious, for I might not be as rich, as famous and as successful as many in and outside the film industry. Then again, this book is not meant for those evolved few, as this wasn't my aim. My dream, hope, desire, passion was always to become an actor and that's what I am today. And I hope some of you reading this book can relate to what I have to say, as I believe that you, like me, want to become an actor, first and foremost. The riches, the success and the fame, I say, would eventually follow. So let's get cracking the code.

1

Flirting with Fame

IT HAPPENED FOR the first time with Channel (V)'s show, *Popstars*. True, it was just casual flirting. There wasn't any commitment from my side and the fidelity was jerky on the other end, too. And none of us felt crummy about it not working out. At least, not back then.

It was the year 2002; I was all of seventeen, in the second year of college pursuing English Honours Never in my wildest dreams had I imagined that I would be selected as one of the top thirty singers in our country and one amongst the three selected from Chandigarh for *Popstars* Season 2. My first brush with fame taught me a lot. And here is where, when I think in retrospect, I discovered one of the many codes that life taught me.

The auditions were happening at Hotel Mountview, Chandigarh, where I stood sweating for my turn for three hours that felt like a decade. But when I entered the venue, I could sense a vibe—a vibe that gave me the confidence, a vibe that didn't make my knees knock, my teeth chatter or my voice tremble. I knew something good was about to happen.

I was ushered by the show's host Purab Kohli into the room where the judges—Palash Sen and Mehnaaz— were sitting. I took one deep breath and sang 'Koi kahe kehta rahe' from the movie *Dil Chahta Hai*, a rage at that time, and also the title song of the movie *Saathiya* for the first round. The results came and I realized I was going for the Mumbai auditions. I was among the top thirty singers from the nation!

I was ecstatic, no doubt, but I knew I wasn't a purist when it came to singing and the only reason I had got selected was because they were looking for a package. I could sing decently, was entertaining enough, and was fairly presentable, too. The last quality of being presentable has a long story to it, which I'll be taking up later in this book.

As far as my selection was concerned, I didn't overestimate myself. I knew where I stood. Barring the pressure of making it to the finals and thinking about charting out a career for myself, I wanted to enjoy the journey. I always knew what I wanted to be and acknowledged the fact that this was a part of my journey. Since I didn't want it to be my destiny, I didn't unnecessarily pressurize myself, and that really helped me live in the moment.

Note to self: The gates to learning open only when the route to self-obsession is blocked.

At that point, without being self-congratulatory, I implemented this philosophy. I was akin to a sponge—ready to take in as much as I could—of Mumbai, music, people and the show *Popstars*. I was myself—real, rough at the edges, not pretentious, earnest. What I didn't know I confessed my ignorance of and sought to learn it from others, and what I knew I seldom spoke of, as intelligence is best exhibited only when put to test by others. It worked. The judges liked me. Perhaps the genuine gullibility is what they liked. Palash (Sen) used to frequently invite me for his events. In fact, post *Popstars*, I was the only contestant who travelled with Purab and Palash to Leh. In short, I guess they liked me and so did destiny.

The contestants of *Popstars* were a buzzing lot. Among my contemporaries was Neeti Mohan, who is still a dear friend. She, too, was a 'complete package'… born to be a star. Cute-looking, a classically trained singer, dancer and a complete dramebaaz to boot. In short, a true rockstar. I always knew she was going to be star—a fact that is now set in stone after she received the RD Burman award for up and coming musical talent at the Filmfare Awards recently! She was the most grounded, too. When she was selected in the top eight along with me, she hugged me and cried her heart out. At that point, I realized two things. One, that what she had was real passion for her art. And two, that this was not my passion, despite being in the top eight just like her and despite the fact that I loved singing and composing songs. And that's when I knew what I had set my heart on.

Vasudha was someone I knew from my college days as a student of our rival college, Hindu, in Delhi. She was a complete natural. She was predominantly into western artistes and played the guitar well. Sangeet was not a great singer but an amazing musician. Jimmy was the oldest in the group and had great energy. He was a decent singer and a fabulous guitarist. These four formed the group, Aasma, and released their first song, 'Chandu ke chacha ne.'

Apart from them, there was Amit Tandon, who later became a Channel (V) VJ and an actor on a GEC (General Entertainment Channel).

Manjari Phadnis later shot to fame as Imran Khan's pretty girlfriend in *Jaane Tu Ya Jaane Na*.

Mansi Parekh became a fabulous actor on a GEC and also won the *Star Ya Rockstar* singing contest.

Surveen Chalwa (also from Chandigarh), the prettiest girl out of the thirty and the youngest of the lot, is now an acclaimed Punjabi actor and has made her debut in Bollywood. She later became a known face of a GEC and will be scorching the big screen soon.

The routine at *Popstars* had us sing innumerable songs every day. The drill started with Mickey Mehta's fitness classes in the morning, followed by singing workshops and sessions. Post that, we were free to do whatever we wanted to. Most of us chilled out till late in the night, but my roomie Jaspreet and I would quietly retire to our room and sleep with an agenda to wake up fresh. But that didn't happen. The sleep part, I mean. I remember being perpetually nervous. I was never confident about myself. Each day was like the last day for me as the eliminations happened after every round. Again, the nervousness was not about reaching the top four. Trust me when I say that it was all about giving a good performance and reaching as far ahead in the journey as possible. It was my first exposure and I truly wanted to make the most of it. In fact, I remember one instance when, in one of the workshop sessions, we were asked to write, sing, compose and choreograph a song. Two opposing teams of five were formed. My group had Neeti and me, amongst the most enthusiastic of the bunch. We not only wrote and composed a song, but also choreographed a dance that turned out pretty well. Since she two of us were the only dancers, we stood out. And we won. The way we bonded, sang and danced, people began to assume there was something brewing between the two of us, despite the fact that everybody knew we were individually in committed relationships. What I felt was this amazing creative energy emanating from her that I latched on to and I feel it was the same for her. It was that wonderful amalgamation of energies that helped us create a beautiful song that won us the round. And then there were others creating waves of controversies.

Physical attraction at such shows is a common phenomenon. Manjari Phadnis and Amit Tandon, the good-looking duo, had definitely something brewing there. Later, of course, they dated for a bit. Again, it was relatively new exposure for a small-town bloke like me.

Speaking of my humble small-town existence, I remember this being the first time I had stayed at a five-star hotel, the Grand Hyatt. It was quite frightful. Among the many other things that we had to manage, there was one particular issue that was disconcerting to both Jaspreet and me. There were no bolts in the washroom! We would in any case be in a state of constant fear for most of the day, and now we couldn't even take a dump without the fear of being indecently exposed! And this was the same hotel where the press conference of my first solo anchored television show, *Music Ka Maha Muqqabla*, was held. It's amazing how life comes a full circle. I truly believe that if you have sown the seeds of desire, there is no way that life wouldn't give you an opportunity to reap the fruits of it. The choice then is personal: whether you want to see those seeds develop or stunt their growth or even uproot them. The choice is always given and the choice is always yours.

Here, I also remember another instance that had hit me hard at the time. There was this contestant called Geet Sagar from Madhya Pradesh. He was one brilliant singer, someone who I was confident would make it to the list of finalists. I was shocked when he was rejected a lot before me. It was honestly depressing. He was extremely talented. And, in a way, I felt guilty. But here the 'code' was operating. A code incomprehensible to my juvenile self at that point of time, a code that I realized existed only after my movie *Nautanki Saala*, a code that I'll talk about later in the book.

The unpredictable twists in *Popstars* took Amit Tandon by surprise, too. I vividly remember the day the results for the top four were announced. Amit was confident about making it. In fact, even before the results were out, he had arranged a cake for himself to be cut later and shared with the rest of us after the obvious decision. He just couldn't come to terms with the fact that he didn't make the cut for the top four. I saw him cry exactly like Neeti. It's amazing how the process of breaking into tears was the same for both of them. The same passion was on display but the emotion was placed on exactly opposite sides of the spectrum.

In all, it was a liberating experience for me. I was surrounded by so much talent that my faith in my dream of becoming an actor was reaffirmed. This experience gave me that ambitious and infectious 'Mumbai' energy. I was awestruck by Mumbai and I knew I had to come back to this city of dreams.

Now here I would also like to take you through another aspect of flirting with fame. It's sweet but it stings too. I studied in an all-boys school, and then in an all-boys college. Never did I get the attention of too many girls except for one person—my then girlfriend and now wife, Tahira. Flooded with the 'proposals' from boys all around, she turned a deaf ear to them, for she was committed to me. In this context, the experience of *Popstars* in Mumbai gave me all that I never had and, in a way, briefly took what I had. To be frank, the female attention, the cool single VJs and the frivolous affairs had a huge impact on me. I was at an impressionable age and was mighty impressed with Mumbai's alluring coolness, so much so that, at one point, I wanted to forget the commitment I had made back home. Now, before you quickly start judging me, give me a chance to tell you about my past. Like I have mentioned earlier, being 'presentable' was one characteristic that I had to struggle with for the longest time ever and it reminds me of my life before *Popstars*.

∎

I remember expressing my love for cinema to my folks when I couldn't even tie my shoelaces. I can never forget the sight of my own self. Born with crooked teeth, flat feet, an ostrich-like jumpy walk, being the shortest in my class and to top it all, being extremely skinny. It was as if my skin didn't like being separated from my bones, so it stuck to it like a faithful lover, leaving no space for fat, the philanderer. In fact, there were no clothes of my size, so my permanent accessory was a belt. My father was perhaps unhappy and even frustrated that I wasn't growing up to be the 'gabru Punjabi jawaan'. Butter, cream, chicken and my mother's desperate prayers—nothing worked.

I was born after five miscarriages—perhaps a reason for both my parents not to give up on me. I was never the one who was cuddled by family friends and I thought that was how it was. Not until the day when arrived another, oh, sorry, the *first* cute baby boy in our family. Fair, round, black-haired, inquisitive-eyed and button-nosed—in short, Aparshakti, my baby brother, straight from a fairytale. I loved him too and was amazed to see what an aunty magnet this little one was. One small squeak from this tiny being initiated a wave of 'awws' and 'cootchie coos' from everybody around. And here I was, with the desire to become an actor with people not even remotely acknowledging me, and even if they did, doing so with remorse and sympathy. I really wanted to tell them that I was still breathing! But, then, who could shut them up? When people came over to see us, they would inevitably remark how the little one was too cute and the elder one 'thoda maada jiya hai'. The literal translation of 'maada' is 'faulty'. Really? Now I was a faulty piece with a manufacturing defect? They advised my parents to feed me better. My father had a tough time trying not to lose his temper. Of course, they fed me and wanted me to gain some weight. But then that's how it is with Punjabi families.

Remarks, comments, unwanted sympathy just came along like influenza. I vividly remember when I was going to be a part of a play in my first grade at St. Stephen's School—I was six. I was extremely excited about it. My excitement levels didn't drop a notch despite knowing the fact that my role required me to just enter and fall clumsily and exit. And I did that with a lot of sincerity. In fact, I had learnt every character's dialogues by heart. I don't know what I was preparing for, but I was. That was the first time my parents had come to see a play. And after seeing my dramatic presence of precisely seven seconds on stage, it was also the last time they saw me on stage. Till date, they haven't seen me perform live.

Then came a time where there was a fancy dress competition. I was seven and my brother five. I became a Manipuri and learnt an entire Manipuri dance sequence by heart and that, too, almost to perfection. My brother, who was just interested in eating and playing, was dressed up as Lord Shiva, who came and callously moved around his 'damroo', and left gawkily. I was quite disappointed with his performance. So when the results came, I was shocked beyond belief. He won the fancy dress competition! It was time for some self-introspection. Being presentable did matter. And, honestly, I realized it at that age itself. (A realization that later made me nail *Popstars*; they weren't just looking for performers; they were looking for complete entertainers, for a package that I forced myself to become). Call it being precocious or giving myself a reality check, but I figured out that looks did matter, which I didn't have back in the day. And I realized that there was no point in self-pity. With my physical attributes at the time, I knew I could never look cute, and even if tried, I would perhaps end up looking like a smiling scarecrow. I needed to work really hard to get noticed. So I decided to use the other facets of my personality. Here, I would like to mention that, all through this while, not once did I undermine myself. I guess I was too mature for my age but it helped.

I decided that the best option for me would be to hone my talent and, yes, also be decently presentable. This is when I first became an entertainer, by mimicking singers/actors/family friends et al. I earned a place for myself in everyone's heart. Based on my 'killer looks', I was part of Hanumanji's 'vaanar sena' in the local ramlila. But the difference was that my entry was much awaited.

'Ab aa rahe hain 482 sector 8 ke Khurrana sahib ke bade ladke, master Ayushmann, Michael Jackson ka dance lekar!' That's exactly what I used to do in front of the gigantic Ravana effigy and the crowds used to go ballistic and cheer for me crazily. My version of Raj Kapoor's 'Mera joota hai japani' was also everyone's favourite. I am not exaggerating here, but the staff of the regular restaurants we went to looked forward to our visits just to see me perform. The same was the case with our family friends, who waited for our family to come over to their houses with much anticipation—so much so that they kept a stick handy just for me to perform my 'Mera joota hai japani' act. Each time my entry was announced—be it at the ramlila, the Sector 17 Saturday carnival, the restaurants or our family friends' get-togethers, I would feel a wave of excitement surge through my body—somewhat like how Alex, the lion, felt in the movie *Madagascar*. And I feel exactly the same even today. The fact that I then became an endearing character for everyone was perhaps because I was genuinely grateful for the applause I got after each performance and bowed in all humility each time. Their love meant a lot to me and I thanked them from the bottom of my heart for appreciating my art. This, and the dimples I inherited from my mom, helped me come across as a nice guy with a promising future.

I had cemented my faith in myself that some day I would become an actor.

Note to self: Know yourself. Respect yourself. Prepare yourself. Make your weakness your strength and supplement your strength with an equal dose of humility.

As I had mentioned in the beginning, my first fling

with fame taught me my first extremely important code. This far into my journey, I was gaining credence as this entertaining, quirky geek. Yes, I did get attention, but predominantly from my batchmates (only boys) or from uncles and aunties. Girls were still not in the picture.

Cut to *Popstars*. Suddenly, I was this cute guy who sang like a dream. Girls began to hit on me. This was a huge leap for me—from being the nerdy guy, almost on the verge of being called 'ugly', to becoming a 'dreamboat'. This became my best trip ever.

Anyway, I was rejected after reaching the top eight. But it didn't hit me hard because it was only fair. Neither was I the best singer nor was that my aim. So I went back home with a whole lot of new experiences, and honestly, some amount of air, too. Despite being a practical, grounded person, I faltered. The fact that I was the first Chandigarh boy to have made it to the top of a major talent show got the better of me. This was when I lost my ground for the first and, I hope, the last time.

When there's no humility, there's enough room for stupidity. So the one stupid thing that I did on reaching Chandigarh was breaking up with the one honest person in my life. And had she not been clear about what we shared, I would have never realized the gravity of my loss. She's always loved me for the person that I was; her affections had nothing to do with the fame that came to me much later.

Two months after returning home, I was back to square one, and this time it was for keeps. One good thing I did was that I continued my singing sessions along with sporadic doses of classical training. I didn't give up because of rejection. I continued learning for my love of the art. And it's a law—true passion without any expectation of result always bears fruit. This laid the groundwork for my journey ahead.

Code #1: *It's essential to value relationships, especially with those who will always be in love with the real, imperfect, juvenile you. Trust me, you wouldn't find many such genuine folk. And the reason I say that this is commitment to self because these are the only people who will time and again, make you meet your real self. And being real is the only key to happiness and success.*

Commitment towards your art or talent is the real passion. You never know when your honest endeavours might pay off. Be prepared; you never know when opportunity comes your way. Had I not pursued singing even after being rejected, 'Paani da rang' wouldn't have happened ten years later. And my life wouldn't have changed. Ten years is a long wait, but if you have no expectations, then it ceases to be frustrating and becomes a beautiful journey instead. It's a pattern. If you are preparing for something, there is no way you wouldn't get a chance to prove yourself. And success is when preparation meets opportunity.

It has happened to me, it has happened to others who have made it, and it will happen to you, too.

2

Main Bhi Hero

LIFE WAS BACK to normal after *Popstars*, albeit with a fair share of fame and recognition. This is when the theatre bug bit me. I was part of DAV College's theatre team called Aaghaaz and we made a name for ourselves at theatre festivals. Rochak Kohli, with whom I later composed 'Paani da rang' was part of this group, too. More often than not, we won the youth theatre festival we were participating in, and reached and won the national round, too. My parents, particularly my father, didn't approve of my theatre stint, for they had a clichéd image of a theatre person in mind: shabbily dressed smokers who drank innumerable cups of tea a day and sat introspecting about life. My explanations didn't change his perception, so I continued doing theatre on the sly. Sometimes it is good to be rebellious if your heart and soul believe in what you do.

Note to self: There is no point being a non-conformist for something for which you have neither the passion nor the understanding—being a rebel without a cause.

After tenth grade, like most other Chandigarh kids, I gave myself a choice between being an engineer and a doctor. Since mathematics didn't like me much, I opted for the medical stream—biology, chemistry and physics, to be precise. They didn't seem to hate me, but could just about tolerate me—enough to let me pass my twelfth grade. As fate would have it, I cleared one of the entrance exams and secured a seat in a dental college. This was the time I seriously thought about my future. Now, had I excelled in the field of medicine, I should have been able to earn myself an MBBS seat. If I didn't excel in it and didn't even have an aptitude for it, would it make any sense trying to prove myself for the rest of my life?

The answer was a big NO. But the realization dawned only after I had proved my mettle in the field of dramatics. Time and again, I was awarded the best actor in theatre circuits and my oratory skills were also highly appreciated. I think it would have been foolish of me to have let go of the BDS seat had I been mediocre at dramatics, too. I think one has to be practical enough to weigh talent and aptitude on an unbiased scale.

■

Since I am in Mumbai now and have faced dilemmas like many of you, I can't help but share with you my observations of the various kinds of people who come to this city with a pocketful of dreams. Some of them are my own distant relatives and friends whose aspirations of becoming stars (yes, I deliberately say 'star' and not 'actor' as they are not even remotely associated with acting) have become stronger after seeing me make it in Bollywood. *'Aae kar sakda hai te assi ki maade haan?!'* (If he can do it, then we can do it better!) is what they have exclaimed far too often.

This is not to ridicule anyone, but perhaps growing up I too thought it was easy to become an actor. You don't need to be educated or acquire any technical qualifications. You just need to do a bit of 'dramebaazi' and develop some rippling muscles. Had it not been a gradual journey for me, which included completing my masters degree, I would have certainly lost the plot.

Coming back to the kind of people thronging Mumbai with the hopes of becoming the next Salman or Shahrukh, I come across many who believe they are incredibly good-looking and extremely talented (in their own eyes). Of course, everyone is special in their own way and confidence goes a long way in this industry, but one should not jump the gun when it comes to self-assumption. My humble request to these people would be to look at themselves from the world's eyes. Put your looks and talent to test. Of course, winning a beauty pageant in a small town with only ten other contestants doesn't really qualify as a test. If, even after getting enough chances to prove yourself, you haven't been able to impress the world, haven't caused it to sit up and take notice, it's time for some self-introspection. There is a possibility that you either don't have an aptitude for it or are not working hard enough. Of course, there are exceptions and you might be doing everything right and success might still evade you, and I am no one to tell you whether or not your ambitions are realistic, but then again, these are my own observations.

Herein comes another breed of people who are extremely talented and yet have been slogging to make it big for years now. I am not kidding; these are not just one or two people, but at least twenty-five to thirty that I know of who have been trying for more than ten years in this industry to make it big. Those who have been around for five-odd years are many, so those who started at twenty-five are thirty today. Of course, there is no set age for being an actor, but one can't evade reality for too long. Just how long can you keep mentioning that you are twenty-two on the audition boards when the people who are auditioning and casting have seen you around for a decade or so! Then, again, I think, is it wrong to aspire towards that goal, especially when you have the aptitude and the talent for it? The answer is NO. Of course, it's not wrong to try for something that you believe is your calling.

But this is when destiny comes in to play. And this is true not only in acting but in life in general. I know so many people who have tried their hardest to get something that they are clearly cut out for but have failed. My friend, Siddarth Kaushal, recently failed in his last attempt to qualify for army selections, despite being the fittest in his school; having an elder brother as a major in the army, too, didn't help. Another cousin of mine slogged it out to clear the civil services exam but couldn't make it, despite having been a topper in school all his life. The examples are endless. If a ten-year time frame was not good enough, there is no point ruining your entire life over it. Sometimes there's no point in fighting your destiny. Perhaps being associated with the desired field in some way or the other can help you understand your potential better and, someday, you never know, you might just crack it. Had I not been an actor, I don't know what would I have been is what I keep telling myself. I earned my way to it by dabbling in various other roles—I was a radio jockey, then a video jockey and later a television anchor. But, each time, I honestly made peace with the circumstances I was in.

Though I always wanted to be an actor, I knew it's not necessary I actually become one. And, even today, I say that it's not necessary that the fame lasts since this industry is extremely fickle. They say you've got only one lifetime and you should spend it chasing your dreams but you can't keep chasing them for the rest of your life and end up becoming a frustrated, bitter human being. What good is your life then?

Coming back to my story, life seemed breezy after I gave up my BDS seat and took up arts with English Honours at DAV College, Chandigarh. I was amongst the very few—okay, to be honest, the only one—of the theatre students who attended a few classes. Somehow education meant a lot to me, and still does.

My batch of Aaghaaz was an amazing, dedicated lot. We used to practise for seventeen hours at a stretch sometimes for youth festivals. The energy was infectious and we were eager learners. This was the first batch in the history of DAV College that stepped out of Chandigarh's cozy cocoon and went on to win competitions at IIT Bombay and BITS Pilani.

Of course, we had our share of rough experiences before we actually got there. The most vivid one was in the year 2002, the first time our college ventured out of its home turf and participated at BITS Pilani's college fest. I was a part of the theatre group as well as the debate team and was super kicked about it.

I think I packed a little more than just the essentials in a modest VIP suitcase that was bursting at its seams, as opposed to the rest of the team that coolly carried around their ultra-light rucksacks. That was a laugh-out-loud moment for many, but I didn't know that the sound of the mockery was ominous and was going to last us the entire trip. There were around twenty of us and our contingent leader was Sunil Bissa, who conveniently made us catch a train to Pilani via Bikaner as he had to meet his parents. Unfortunately, we came to know about his personal agenda much later (for which we beat him up). But the damage was done instead of a nine-hour journey, we would reach Pilani in just about twenty-four hours! Since he was our leader we couldn't do much as the rest of the trip depended on him, so we quietly made peace with the aloo puri we were fed at his home in Bikaner and the rickety bus ride that almost broke our backs enroute to Pilani. To drown our sorrows, we started singing in the bus but were made to shut up by the conductor. The silence accentuated our aches along with the cracking sound of our bones. Thanks to Mr Bissa, we reached Pilani the next night...and, boy, was it worth it!

This was the first time we had shared a campus with pretty girls! My mind was blown away, obviously not just by the mere sight of the girls but the kind of camaraderie the girls and boys shared. It was beyond anything I had ever experienced. They were chatting, having heated discussions, painting, singing, jamming, smoking up and, of course, some were making out, too. It was our first experience of life outside our college and we realized that it could consist of a lot more than student politics, swords, Punjabi swear words and the 'geri route'. (Those who don't know the geri route, wait for my next book! Actually, anyone from Chandigarh can write a thesis on it! And I'll be surprised and disappointed if the term doesn't make it to the Oxford dictionary soon. It does have a Wikipedia entry, though.)

This was the first time we heard rock bands live. Trust me when I say that for those few days, we Chandigarh boys had our brows perpetually touching our hairlines as we witnessed so many new things. The jamming sessions and rock bands were something we had seen only on MTV and Channel V. The debate competition didn't go too badly and I was among the top five participants.

But what turned out to be the most humiliating experience was our street play. We didn't really know what went into a street play but since we were the best in our city ('frogs in a pond' is the idiom that comes to mind here) we were confident we could manage it. This, of course, was crushed to tiny pieces later on. We had converted a popular stage play called *Toya* into a street play format. But this was not the reason behind our being at the receiving end of a mass mockery session. It was our uber cool dress code. Since it was our first exposure to the outside world, we had wanted to make a lasting impression. Last it did, but definety not in the way we wanted it to. We were dressed in black trousers and crisp, white, full-sleeved shirts for a street play! We thought we had done a brilliant job. But as we looked around at the crowd from colleges like Hindu and KMC, Delhi, we realized that some of them looked like waiters and some like underfed cricket umpires. It would be an understatement to say that we were shit intimidated by those wearing jeans and kurtas. They had confidently slung scarves around their necks and went around dancing and interacting with the audience during their act.

We were overawed and, of course, they were over-entertained by our not-so-intentional buffoonery. Needless to say, the girls we wanted to impress the most were smirking at us and, by the end of the festival, we became girl repellants.

Anyway, after this highly enlightening and humiliating experience, it was time to come back, home. Simpletons we may have been but we were not losers. So, the next year we went to IIT Bombay's fest, where we once again met the same teams from Hindu and KMC college. In fact, I first met Vasudha (a member of the band Aasma, a product of *Popstars*) at these fests. She was from Hindu college. Anyway, this time we presented a play called *Lohe Ka Swaad,* and it was critically acclaimed.

But this wasn't enough for us, so we came back the next year with another play called *Mann Ki Bhadaas,* a musical. And from being a bunch of losers out of their depth, we went on to win the first prize, beating the same people who had once mocked us. The small-town kids that we were, we couldn't control the tears of joy that came flooding from our eyes. As I write this, my eyes still get moist when I remember the experience. We couldn't sleep the entire night due to our excitement.

Among the many memorable experiences, I can recollect one more—my audition day at Aaghaaz. The rest of the team, including Rochak, was already a part of the theatre group. Then came my audition and I was introduced as Rochak's friend. I was made to deliver the lines of Rochak's character. The end result was that I got the role and he was strangely moved backstage. It was funny at that time, and it didn't affect our relationship one bit.

There was another incident where I literally attacked my friend Vikas Sharma's manhood—not deliberately, of course. It was during one of the youth festivals organized at Chandigarh's MCM College for girls. We were staging a play called *Kumara Swami* where I was playing the title role, and blame it on my lenses or my bad (or good, depending on your point of view) aim that I nearly castrated Vikas in a sword fighting sequence. Funny as it may sound now, back then it was quite tragic and the poor guy managed to perform despite getting stitches in his...ahem...sensitive area.

I belonged to an amazing batch and the best part is that all the people in my group have come on their own. Puneet Khanna is a chief assistant director; Ravi Yuvraj Panthi an ex-army officer; Sameer Kaushal a guitarist who is also a major in the army; Rochak Kohli a music composer; Charandeep Kalra an editor and producer; Aviral Gupta a businessman and still a theatre enthusiast; and Vikas Sharma an assistant director. When I see my friends doing well in their fields, it gives me immense happiness and I hope this story becomes an inspiration for many to make the most of their talent.

While in college, all of us were actors but life took its course and all of us chose what best fitted us—according to our personalities, our aptitudes and above all, our destinies. The best example is that of my army buddy Sameer, who has staged many short plays in his army circles and is a hit at all parties thanks to his mimicking and guitar-playing skills. Aviral, who is a successful businessman in Chandigarh, once aspired to be an actor but couldn't make it to Mumbai because of circumstances. Yet, he didn't let the artist in him die; he is playing the lead protagonist in a one-act play written and directed by my wife, Tahira, and they have been successfully staging it across the country these days.

The crux of the matter is that one has to be honest to one's passion. Be it gardening, cooking, acting, teaching, sculpting, pottery or academics; if the circumstances are not congenial to promoting your talent, then you must create that environment yourself. You could be a doctor to the world but a potter at home. You could be an army officer at the battlefield but an ace guitarist among your friends. You could be a dentist at work but a dramatist in front of your son. The idea is to derive satisfaction by making an endeavour to not let your passions die.

Code #2: *Here, the code lies in recognizing the path life has charted out for you and doing that within a stipulated time frame. I have seen many lives go waste and it is extremely heartbreaking to see young people wander aimlessly while remaining irrationally hopeful. I feel that the code lies in being pragmatic along with being emotionally idealistic.*

3

Roadie Rathore

THEN CAME THE year 2005, the year of 'Teri maa *#@###', 'Tu saale *$#%@@'. You guessed it right—the year of MTV *Roadies*. I was in the first year of my masters course in mass communication and journalism, when *Roadies* came to Chandigarh. My audition tape is available online as proof of my story of being an ugly duckling! Not that I am a swan today, but definitely better off than the uni-browed, stickly, ghastly figure that I was back then! I still don't know what made them select me—perhaps the fact that their abuses just bounced off me, or maybe the fact that I was like a jester in their court who could mimic, sing and entertain everyone. For whatever reason, I am just glad they did.

However, the story of how I landed there is an interesting one too. I had auditioned for a television serial by Balaji Telefilms called *Kitni Mast Hai Zindagi*, the first fiction show on MTV, which didn't do so well. However, I was noticed in that audition but, to my surprise, by the *Roadies* team in Mumbai. I remember when I got a call from Mumbai I was attending a lecture and had to bury my head under the desk and take the call. I was super excited when I recognized a Mumbai number.

'Hi, I'm Raghu,' said the voice on the other end. At that time, Raghu wasn't 'The Raghu'. And I had the audacity to ask, 'Who Raghu?' Not many had seen him on television yet. He asked me to audition for *Roadies* but I wasn't interested. That kind of show didn't suit my aspirations. After all, I wanted to be an actor. Raghu told me to think about it and get back to him. When I told my father he said, 'Zaroor jao' (You should definitely go). I still don't know what my father foresaw, but he pushed me into it. At that time, I was rehearsing for my theatre group Manch Tantra's production called *Painter Babu*, in which I was playing the lead.

I told my group about my audition. They dissuaded me to such an extent that I almost dropped the thought of going to the audition. But I knew I had to go and, in retrospect, I'm glad I did.

> **Code #3:** *Never let go of an opportunity. If it comes knocking at your door, it's worth giving your hundred per cent to at least once. It worked in my case.*

My stint in *Roadies* was a game-changer for me. Not because I went on to win it but because I met a man named Raghu who, in a way, has been my guardian angel. Perhaps he doesn't know it or is too humble to acknowledge it but, from the day he met me, he has invariably been a guiding light to me on my journey. Be it *Roadies*, Big FM or MTV, this 'tor-mentor' has always been there for me.

Coming back to my *Roadies* audition. My aspiration had always been to become an actor and, heeding my father's advice, I thought perhaps this would take me closer to my primary goal. And this is how I reached Hotel Sea Princess in Mumbai.

The auditions were taking place on the top floor. I was quite intimidated when I reached there. The place was buzzing with super fit and good-looking guys. Some were flexing their muscles, others were doing push-ups, while the rest were just basking in their naturally good looks. My efforts in looking presentable seemed quite vain in front of those six-footers. But later I realized that *Roadies* was not about biceps or quadriceps.

The people selected to be on the show were shortlisted solely on Raghu's discretion. It could be a kink in a person, some eccentricity, entertainment quotient or sheer courage. No one knew who could make the cut. I'm glad I made it. Apart from me, the *Roadies 2* team comprised Neha, Shaleen, Candy, Vinod and Varun. We were asked to make one last call to our folks before heading towards a forty-day ordeal with no communication with the outside world whatsoever. Somehow, when this journey came to an end, my emotions were pretty much the same as they were in the beginning. I am a fairly detached person, a fact that came out when the show ended and everyone else was misty-eyed about leaving. Aastha cried incessantly while I was only too glad to be heading back home, away from the absolute madness.

To be honest, I would never have taken part in such a daring reality show had it not been for my ambition to become an actor. Those who watched *Roadies 2* would agree that the place was not for me. Neither was I a part of the bitching sessions nor was

I some 'faadu' task accomplisher. In fact, at some tasks, the girls were way better than me.

I remember a task where we had a military route to follow and had to cross hurdles in minimum time. One such task had all of us climbing a wall. I was only concentrating on the bespeckled radar in front of me. My father's guru mantra, which taught one to concentrate at the current piece of work to an extent that the surrounding objects and distractions blurred away, was resounding in my head. And I was at this task as if I was going to beat the shit out of everyone. The concentration and focus required were immense. What broke the tension was the sound of a few giggles. And as I tore away from the unified coordination that existed perfectly between my limbs, my gaze and the wall, I observed that I was the last person struggling to climb up.

Anyway, I think I lasted the vote-outs because I was never too conspicuous or threatening to anyone as far as politics, tasks, bitching sessions, link-ups or break-ups were concerned. And that stuff didn't interest me much either. But when it came to the singing sessions around the bonfire, or pulling the other contestants' legs in good humour, I was a front-runner. In a way, I won *Roadies 2* not for being the best Roadie but perhaps for just being the real Ayushmann. I couldn't be pretentious at all and there was no point to it either. The moment you deviate from being yourself, you become a wannabe. And then there is no escaping Raghu's wrath.

In fact, I think Raghu was like a painfully honest mirror. He just showed you what you really were. Beyond his onscreen 'assassinator' image was this immensely talented person who I really connected with. He loved to sing and had an eye and appreciation for creativity and artists. In fact, it was during that time that I first made him hear Rochak's and my composition, 'Paani da rang'. I think he quite liked it. To sum it up, the entire *Roadies* journey was a learning step for me. I can't begin to think of any situation that didn't teach me something for keeps. Deep down, I knew that after those forty brutal days I was a much wiser person, though I still had a long way to go. Needless to say, the process of growing up is never-ending.

■

Some of the tasks on *Roadies* Season 2 were really crazy. At least they were for me. This one task was really embarrassing where we had to wear only langots (underwear) and wrestle with professional wrestlers.

Those voted by the other Roadies had to fight and since no one had a problem with me, I wasn't chosen to fight. Nonetheless, a bespectacled broomstick wearing a chaddi sitting at the periphery of the wrestling arena still garnered more attention than those who were actually fighting. In retrospect, I made quite a sight I suppose, so I can't blame them!

If the above task had me embarrassed, the next one made me pensive. We were in Punjab and had to live the rural life. We drove tractors, did 'kheti baadi', bathed in fresh, cold tubewell water and cooked food from whatever we collected. Only Candy and I could speak with the locals there as the villagers spoke chaste Punjabi. From where we stayed, I could see the border, and knew that, at times, the locals unknowingly drifted into Pakistan.

I saw no man's land. And as I looked up, I saw birds flying past the borders without any passport, security checks or sparking the suspicion of the authorities. It was a surreal moment for me. I often wondered if the birds had their nests in Pakistan and came over to the Indian side to look for food. It might sound crazy, but I honestly spent hours looking at the border and the birds.

Among the many incidents that I can never forget

is the one where we donated sperm at a sperm bank in Allahabad. I entered a room splashed with slogans of infertility and assisted reproduction. And these pamphlets stuck on the wall surely weren't giving me a hard on. There was a bathroom attached to it and there were no porn DVDs to encourage us, like in my film, *Vicky Donor*. I left it to my wild imagination. The rest is history. All the boys took up the challenge except for Shaleen, who backed out.

Deep down, I felt like I had done a good thing. Perhaps a childless couple would be blessed with a bundle of joy. And, trust me, we felt quite happy when we were told the next day that our samples were virile enough to be selected. For me, it wasn't a boost to my ego but more of a reassurance that I had helped somebody. I think I would have never been able to say yes to a stupendous script like *Vicky Donor*, which was refused by many actors, had this episode not happened to make me understand the importance of sperm donation.

Code #4: *This code lies in being receptive to what life has to offer. It could be a tragedy, an embarrassing situation, a hilarious one, a sad one or an elating one. There is something to understand and take away from every experience.*

The controversies didn't stop. There were numerous make-out sessions between my co-contestants. And another incident which perhaps will not be easily erased from our memories was when Candy stepped out in a bikini. I was a very anxious pillion ridder, but I only sat behind Candy because she had a great butt, and I bet she knew the reason and had no issues with it. So it was all cool. The long journeys seemed to get over in mere minutes. I guess boys will be boys! The tasks were endless and so were the mind games. We were made to drive for hours continuously with limited sleep and then put in situations that would make us susceptible to losing our minds. What gave me strength along the way was my wit and sense of humour.

Two months later, after public voting, I was announced the winner of *Roadies* Season 2. Back home, everyone was ecstatic. Five lakh rupees meant a lot and that, too, for a young student. I got a Karizma bike, too. I think the fact that I was neither pretentious nor ultra cool made the public vote for me. Then again, Punjabis are known for their open-heartedness, which is probably why their votes came in abundance.

So here I had a choice. I could have utilized the fame and shifted to Mumbai right away (as some people put it, to strike the iron when it was hot) or I could continue with my masters degree and finish it. I chose the latter—not because I desired to particularly excel in academia, but because I knew that further education was important. If not anything else, it gave me time to mature in a safe cocoon. Those who become delusional with fame and success and compromise their learning years can lose touch with reality very easily. And I say this since I have seen the television industry, and can safely say that ninety percent of the television fraternity, especially actors, live in a bubble.

4

Main Struggler Hoon

FINALLY, MY POSTGRADUATION days came to an end, along with my daily routine of gorging samosas dripping with sweet red chutney at our canteen. The days at the university were beautiful but, sadly, numbered. I had big plans for myself. I had charted it all out meticulously. After my last exam, there was to be just a week of rest followed by horse riding and swimming classes, hardcore gyming while following a diet plan to help me beef up, and occasional theatre workshops.

Finally, the exams got over and, like any other relieved student, I celebrated it with friends by chilling over mugs of beer and lemonade (beer for my friends and lemonade for me. Yes, I have always been and still am a teetotaler) while discussing our future plans. Sameer was set to shift to Delhi to join a multinational company. Rohini was going to continue running her family business of designing and printing. Tahira had plans of opening her own public relations company which she did from the very next day, and Karanbir Bedi, who was an adventure freak, wanted to do something along those lines.

Karanbir later shifted to Pune and started writing for *Overdrive* magazine. I blatantly told everyone about my plans of making it as an actor. Sameer and Bedi guffawed while Rohini looked at Tahira with eyes full of pity. And as for Tahira herself, well, she wasn't really stunned because she never believed my aspirations were for real. She didn't take cognizance of the fact that anyone with a ghastly stick figure for a body could aspire to join Bollywood. Well, what are the odds!

As I reached home in the evening, I saw packed luggage at the doorway. It looked like someone was shifting for at least a month. I was the one being shoved out. My father literally threw me out of the house to go make it big in Mumbai, crushing to pieces my plans of following the impeccable schedule I had prepared for myself. My father is an astrologer, and according to his calculations, this was an apt period for a transition in my life. With a lot of convincing, I was able to buy just one more day after which my ticket to Mumbai was bought.

That day was just for my girl, Tahira. That was our last date before I left my home town to chase my dreams. I vivdly remember that date at the parking lot of CITCO, our hangout spot. I had nothing to tell her about where I would stay, whom I'd meet, when I'll come back. There was just one thing I was sure about: that I was going to Mumbai the next day, perhaps and hopefully, forever. There were no promises made except for the fact that I would always be loyal to her and that she'd wait for me.

In retrospect, that day was quite filmy. She cried a lot. There was so much uncertainty over my career. She was fearful either way my career turned out. What if I didn't become an actor? Even she knew that all I had ever done was nautanki. And worse, what if I became an actor; what would she tell her family of journalists, bureaucrats and educationalists? They would never agree to our marriage.

Like I said, that was our last date before I left and then I met her exactly after two years, only to get engaged to her. Technology wasn't as commonplace then, so communication was not easy. There was no

Facebook or Skype, but thankfully mobile phones soon became popular, especially with free incoming charges.

Thus, with a gloomy heart and an ambitious soul, I reached Mumbai and headed to my friend Karan's place in Kandivili straight from the station. I had requested him to let me stay for a couple of days before I managed to find decent accommodation but he, being the Punjabi that he was, offered to let me stay for as long as I wanted. When I reached his place, the door was opened by a girl I knew from Chandigarh— his girlfriend, Smita. I was very happy for them when I saw that they had each other's support in a place like Mumbai. But what I didn't know was that, in his one-room flat, he had her permanent company, too. Everything seemed just fine until the sun went down and I was made to sleep with them on their bed. Of course, Karan lay between us, but I couldn't sleep a wink, knowing what was going on right beside me. It still remains one of the most uncomfortable nights of my life. The next day I left hurriedly, with no place to go.

This is when I called up another friend, Siddharth Kapathia. He was pursuing MBBS from KEM Hospital, Lower Parel, and he snuck me into his hostel by making me wear a lab coat all day long. And it ended up being a lot of fun! All the doctors became my friends and I became the clown of the hostel. I had always wanted to experience hostel life and got the chance to do so soon after reaching Mumbai, the city where dreams are realized. I remember all the boys at the hostel sleeping in just their underwear, and three boys having to share one room. Kapathia's roommate had a problem with me staying there, but my doc buddy fought with him and I stayed on for a whole month.

The campus had a hostel mess and a gym that no one went to. Doctors never get the time for such activities. But I was a permanent fixture there. The coach loved me and I was his favourite student, not that he had much of a choice, as I was his only student. It was an old-school Maharashtrian gym, where one had to take off their shoes outside. Also, we had to first bow and pay reverence to Lord Hanuman before starting the regime. It was sort of like a mandir (a 'body temple', to employ a fancier term) with incense sticks and idol worshipping.

But I loved every bit of my life at KEM. Every day was an adventure. The fear of getting caught, the lab rounds, fooling around and entertaining the intelligentsia...the memories of those days still make me smile.

■

My friends were, and still are, mostly small-towners, perhaps because, deep down, I still am one, too. But let me correct myself here—my friends have always been small towny 'characters'. I remember Dr Jha from Benaras Hindu University (BHU), a humble guy. My association with him was revolved around this one question he asked me almost repeatedly every day: he could never fathom why I came in a 'jahaaz' (airplane) to Mumbai! If there was an emergency, he could still justify the airplane in his mind, but no urgency meant no airplane journeys and that was that for him. 'Aap jahaaz se aaye?' is what he kept asking me.

Contrary to their stereotypical, boring image, the doctor as at KEM were super fun. I remember the time when we went to watch Hrithik Roshan's movie *Lakshya* at a single screen theatre. The doctors were so excited while watching the movie; in fact, one of them, Dr Raju Singh, kept saying 'yes, yes, c'mon!' with so much earnestness that, instead of cringing, I backed him up. We used to play cricket on the tennis courts in campus. One of the doctors (whose name I have forgotten now) had a crush on the most beautiful girl on campus. To help him impress her, he was made to face easy bowling that helped him hit sixes each time she crossed us. I don't know if he ended up with that girl, though!

Our favourite hangout spot was this bar-cum-restaurant called Madira (a name that's pretty self-explanatory) where all the doctors would go to drink at night. It was located right outside the MTV office, and was a hot spot for those guys to hang out as well. Who knew that MTV would be my future office!

Then, one day, I called Raghu, the only link I had in this city through *Roadies*. I was really interested in VJing, which was just another chance to be onscreen. Life had taught me over time to respect each stage of my career and to give up on assumptions.

Obviously, I wasn't ready for the screen, so Raghu gave me his friend Nirupam's number for RJing. But, before this, he also gave me a television director's contact number. In those days, I carried my portfolio around—fifty envelopes with fifty profiles that Sameer Bains, my friend from university, had designed for me. Those were the days of hard copies. But no one took me seriously, perhaps because I never looked or behaved like an actor.

I went to Riddhi Siddhi Apartments, a name I found slightly weird, which is why I still remember it, to meet the director and show him my portfolio. But I guess it was only Raghu who had been taking me seriously, and that too only now, after *Roadies* had ended. During the show, I had told him that I wanted to be an actor and he had said, 'Tu kyon apni zindagi barbad karna chahta hai?' Then immediately after *Roadies* was done, I gave auditioned at Channel V to become a VJ. Anirbhan Bhattacharya, the then EP (executive producer) at Channel V, told me (and I remember his exact words), 'Ek aur ghar barbaad...'

So, like I said, no one took me seriously, but the second time I came to Mumbai after my postgraduation, Raghu acknowledged me and said, 'Now you are ready.' Perhaps the two years did help me evolve. This is when Raghu gave the director's number but, of course, that didn't work out. I then called Nirupam, who was the national programming head of Big FM.

On my way to the Big FM office to give my radio interview, I met another man who had come for the interview and was an actor from the National School of Drama. He told me he was going for a Balaji Telefilms audition post the interview. I asked if I could come along, too. He refused point blank, saying that only those who had received a call from them were allowed to audition. He then sat in an auto and zipped away. I decided that I could either sulk or do something about it. And I did.

I hailed another auto and told him to follow the auto in front of us. We reached Balaji. I gave the audition, and guess what? I was selected and he wasn't. Pretty filmy, but then that's Mumbai for you. Anything can happen here. Later, I got a call from Balaji but this was after I had been selected by Big FM and was training to become an RJ at MICA, Ahmedabad. I think I was selected for the role that eventually went to Pulkit Samrat in the epic soap opera *Kyunki Saas Bhi Kabhi Bahu Thi*.

I had to make a decision. It was a choice between becoming a known face on television or just a voice on a radio station. No doubt, the former was extremely luring, but I was really enjoying the stint at MICA, and perhaps the two years of extra wisdom I had gained during my masters had taught me the virtue of patience and helped me understand my shortcomings. I knew I was still an amateur for television.

Note to Self: Outgrow and prove your mettle for one medium before jumping on to the other. This way, not

only will you gain experience but also earn the respect
of the other medium and, materialistically speaking,
definitely earn yourself a higher package later on.

This was the time when FM had just stepped into the
Indian market and was booming everywhere. My dad
always told me that no job was big or small; it was
better to earn your living than be dependent someone
else. So since TV wasn't happening (the Balaji offer
coincided with the radio offer which I had already
taken up) and films were a distant, blurry dream, I
was ready to do anything. I convinced myself to give
my best to whatever came my way.

This is also when my above-mentioned self-note
got further cemented in my head. I knew I just
couldn't sit around in Mumbai's Aaram Nagar (the
hub for struggling actors) giving auditions every day.
That couldn't be my job profile. Of course, having
something in hand and then going for auditions made
more sense.

I still marvel at the young boys and girls that
flood the audition gates of Aaram Nagar every day—
and that's their job! From ten in the morning to six
in the evening (sometimes even longer), that's what
they do, perhaps living off either their savings or the

money their folks keep sending them every month. With due respect to those who follow this routine, I would certainly get depressed if I were in their place. Struggling endlessly and aimlessly to become an actor wasn't my cup of tea. I made up my mind to test myself and earn respect in my own eyes by proving my talent in other mediums till the time people started considering me worthy enough for the medium I had always aspired for.

I got a lot of flak for auditioning for radio and ultimately going to MICA for training. People told me that I was wasting my golden years—this was the time to focus solely on auditions. They said that my acting would improve this way. Really? Somehow this theory didn't work for me. If at all I was deemed fit for movies, I would have been considered at least once in the twenty-odd auditions that I had given. So either I was not meant for it or I wasn't completely ready for it. Since I was not willing to go with the former reason, I convinced myself that it was the latter. Moreover, I needed time to prepare. So I thought I might as well channelize those energies (those that I saved for auditions) into something that would help me evolve, become more talented, and give me exposure.

This reinforced Code #2 for me, which is to be pragmatic along with being emotionally idealistic. And I chose to work in a field (radio jockeying) close to my aspired area of interest. I knew I could only gain and grow from here, which I did in abundance. The reason I could prepare my own links innovatively at MTV, host events and interview celebrities on TV without shaky knees was because I had done all this way too many times, in fact, almost every single day in of my two years in radio.

Anyway, even with radio, it was not as if the world was waiting for me with open arms. The ball wasn't in my court and I knew the privilege of being an RJ wasn't exactly a choice I would get to make. I had cleared the auditions at Mumbai, and now the training at MICA would either seal my fate as an RJ or it would send me back to... I don't know where I would have gone. This was precisely the reason why I put my hundred per cent into this as well. Though being an RJ was never my dream, yet I knew that I had to be good, not just good but par excellence, so that people from the industry would be forced to sit up and take notice of a humble artist called Ayushmann.

The training-cum-workshop at MICA decided whether or not we would get jobs at the end of a two-month programme. If we *were* selected then, according to our performance, we would be placed in A, B, C or D tier cities. The cities were graded according to how big or small the station would be. The first station was to be set up in Delhi, followed by Mumbai and so on. According to my last count, the channel had roughly sixty-two stations across the country. It was a mighty big company to be a part of. Again, like with *Popstars* and *Roadies*, I didn't stress too much over devising any strategy or putting up a façade that would appease the teachers at MICA. I just did what I liked, and I made sure I not just liked but loved and worshipped my work. There wasn't a single day when I was complacent. Each day I prepared, I learnt and I delivered.

Every day at MICA, we had to prepare links according to the topics that were given to us. Essentially, 'links' mean the 'crap' (according to listeners) that an RJ speaks on radio for which they prepare for hours together. What helped me come up with decent links each day was my childhood habit of completing my homework as soon as I came back from school. The rest of my routine of playing, eating and sleeping followed thereafter. And that's precisely what I did at MICA, too. After a tiresome day at training, instead of retiring back to bed like some or hanging out at the canteen like others, I went straight to the library to prepare links for the next day. I would practise these links at least five times out loud in my room to get the enunciation right once my roommate, Pankaj bhai, was away. The beautiful, green campus was a perfect creative zone for me.

There was one interesting feature of this campus: Roxy. He was the principal's pet dog who had this invincible air about him along with a license to enter any classroom in the middle of any lecture and sit beside any student. He would inevitably be roaming around in some classroom or the other instead of wandering outside, since the rooms were air-conditioned. I found this fascinating at first, amusing after a bit, and routine by the end of it.

Then there was this chhota canteen that was open 24X7 and had the most amazing Maggi. Most of the trainees used to spend most of their nights at this canteen, wake up in the morning, quickly jot down some lousy links and then sleep during the sessions. I, on the other hand, was very disciplined, even if to the extent of being boringly so. I completed my six hours of sleep everyday and, come what may, the lights in my room would go off by 11 p.m.

Our classrooms were like huge amphitheaters and we had the best trainers coming in to train us from across the globe. Programming and creative heads flew in from Kiss FM, US, and Capital Radio, UK, to conduct intense workshops with us. Amongst the popular Indian hosts, Gaurav Kapoor was our trainer, too.

Among my batchmates, I got along best with Pankaj Sharma, who was also my roommate. He was from Shimla and a struggling actor in Mumbai. We bonded really well and stayed in Silver Oaks, the newest hostel in MICA. We were the clowns, the entertainers of our batch. We put up mock, impromptu fashion shows in the hostel corridors. The hostels were co-ed, so Pankaj bhai used to act like a stud and was perpetually surrounded by girls.

The fashion show would be conducted to the song, 'Bada samajhaya tennu', a Punjabi song that he plays on air till date, dedicating it to me each time. Pankaj is a popular RJ in Chandigarh today; in fact, I would like to take the liberty to crown him the number one RJ in Chandigarh.

There is this interesting episode about this girl (I've forgotten her name now) who was always planning to run away with her boyfriend, who was in Ahmedabad. She was studying in MICA and her parents were settled abroad. But I got to know later that she cancelled her plan to elope after seeing me. Yes, girls took a fancy to me, too, and apparently this one had a huge crush on me! Ironically, I got to know this from Shruti, another student at MICA, when she was helping me buy a suit for Tahira at the local mall.

Then there was Shalu didi, who was extremely sweet. Shalu didi, as I fondly call her, took care of me like a mother when I was down with viral fever. She, too, could have caught it from me it and that could have adversely affected her links, which was equally proportionate to losing her job. But no sir, she didn't fret; she took care of me day in and day out, till the time I was up and about. I will never forget her kindness. In fact, she used to, in an age-old adorable fashion, take 'nazar' off me. She had a typical South Indian way of doing it.

My batchmates were extremely talented and some were tough competition, too. Siddanth Sagar from Delhi was naturally talented, but not necessarily a hard worker. He later got a job with Big FM, but because of his erratic behavior, indiscipline and a showdown with the programming head, he left.

Rohit Hippalgaonkar from Mumbai was very talented and conventionally good-looking. He, too, was a strong competition. Today he is an RJ with Radio City in Mumbai, doing his own evening show. Now I shall keep my humility aside for a bit and tell you that I used to get the maximum applause for my daily links. There was a community station, called MICA Vaani, and we used to do shows on it with the local villagers playing the part of our callers.

I remember I was to give my first link on the radio, and I was very nervous. With a lot of apprehension and skepticism about my performance, I delivered the link. And no sooner had I finished, there was a roar of applause from my teammates! It was a big high, and the most amazing feeling. Trust me, I didn't feel this way even after *Vicky Donor*. In fact, the response was so positive that even the South Indians who didn't understand Hindi well were clapping enthusiastically for me. It was really rewarding for me to get appreciated time and again by sixty students who didn't know me, who came from different cultures, who were my competitors, but still truly appreciated my art.

I reiterate that all this didn't come naturally to me like it did for some. I was always prepared, and that's the difference. Till date, I rehearse and rehearse like a maniac. Be it a press conference, a radio interview (that I now give and not the other way round), events or film shoots, I prepare every day of my life. Tahira and Rani (my manager) are two people who know of this eccentric side to me. I have no qualms in accepting that I am a hard-working, prepared actor. And by doing this knowingly or unknowingly, I was and still am following the first code.

■

By now, the days, of grueling training sessions were coming to an end, which meant serious business—getting jobs in the real world. Lance, an ex-airforce officer, was the HR head at Big FM. He came to the campus, openly declaring that the salaries against the grades that each one of us got would be awarded after a personal interview with him. The grades were as follows: B which would fetch a salary of ₹18,000; B+ would bring ₹25,000; A would deserve ₹40,000; and an A+ would get you ₹60,000.

Before the final round with Lance, there was another one with Tarun Katyal, the taskmaster and the COO of Big FM. We had to deliver impromptu links in front of him, which, trust me, can be extremely nerve wrecking. He asked me about my background and my aspirations. I told him honestly that I wanted to become an actor. He said, 'Don't worry, I'll make sure you become one.' And I have a story about this too, which will come in later.

In one of the links, I said 'Churchgate se Kalian, Big FM pe Ayushmann'. The team was so impressed with it that they used this example in every presentation of theirs. A trainee marking the entire map of a city to which he didn't even belong and establishing a local connect in just a statement was quite impressive for them. I was already popular in the head office even before joining them.

Well, now came in Lance with his second round of interviews, where he declared the grades and the salaries. Some looked dissappointed after stepping out of his office, while quite a few were happy, too. I didn't know what my fate had in store for me. I went inside and Lance looked up and asked me in typical reality show style, 'What do you think your grade will be?' I said A+, and he raised his eyebrows, clearly taken aback. Was he shocked at my audacity? Or was it disbelief? Anyway, he gave me an envelope and asked me to open it. I did as I was told, thanked him and went outside without asking or saying anything else.

Immediately after stepping out, I called Tahira and asked her to guess my salary. The maximum she could think of was ₹20,000. I asked her to step it up a little. She was already so elated—anything more than ₹20,000 meant a huge deal, as that was the maximum pay packet that was given to any fresher in this field at that time. In fact, if I am not mistaken, only one other person from our batch of forty-five bagged this salary. When she scaled up her guess to 30k, I grinned and asked her to go higher. 'More than 30?!' she squealed. By now she thought I was just faffing as, in her own innocent world, nobody could ever draw such a salary, let alone 'go higher' than that. So she finally gave up. When I told her that I got a grade of A+ and that meant ₹60,000, I was greeted by silence and then incessant screams. That was a particularly memorable moment for the both of us. And I believe that was the last time we discussed money as such. One always remembers their first crush, their first love, their first job and definitely their first salary.

5

Meri Awaaz Suno

SO HERE I was, stationed in Delhi as the highest paid RJ. Delhi was the first station to be launched, which is why I was assigned there, and also because I had more of a Punjabi connect. Not that I had a swagger, but yes, I definitely had a cheerful bounce in my step. (The bounce soon turned into a dribble, soon flattened out and then I was dragging myself to the station everyday, but more on this transition later.)

When I joined, I was given the evening show for which I made my own tagline: 'Maan na maan main, tera Ayushmann', which eventually became synonymous with my name. I was doing well, too, with my show featuring amongst the top five radio shows in Delhi, but I had my eye on the coveted morning show (also known as the breakfast show) which was the most sought-after one, as the first show is always assumed to be the face of the station.

Anyway, my show got maximum attention from everyone in office—including the sales team, programming team, the CEO and, of course, the listeners. One day, after wrapping up my evening show, I retired to my flat, dead tired. During those days, I never kept my phone on silent. At 4 a.m., I got a call from Manav Dhanda, the station head. I was extremely tired and could have just slept off, as I had just finished my work and had no business attending work-related calls in the dead of the night, but I picked up.

A small interjection here: Big 92.7 FM does pay you well, but it sucks the bloody life out of you! When I picked up the call, I came to know that there was an emergency in the office as the breakfast show jockey had fallen sick. Manav asked me if I could fill in; I immediately said yes, and reached the office within an hour to prep for the show.

The show went extremely well, and that seemingly 'silly' action of picking up the phone and not letting an opportunity pass (even though my body had practically given up) had given me the 'breakfast show'. So, the first voice to resonate in office and to be heard by listeners on Big 92.7 FM that day was mine. Big Chai, the breakfast show, was mine.

Code #5: *I can't really elaborate on this one. It is as direct as it gets: NEVER LET GO OF AN OPPORTUNITY!!*

I treated every day as my first and last day at the job. My show eventually became one of the top three shows in Delhi. I shared a good rapport with my CEO, Tarun Katyal, who was fond of me. There was a senior of mine who was actually a young girl, who had the hots for me. It was funny how, at times, she would unassumingly brush past me, or rub her hand lightly on my shoulder; she even told me once that I should have a girlfriend. When I told her that I had one back in Chandigarh, she suggested I should have one in Delhi, too! I managed to keep a straight face and obediently nodded my head. But I wondered what was really going on in her head. In fact, one day Manav, too, asked me if I had a girlfriend in Delhi and if not, he suggested I get one. Honestly, the world didn't help me much in remaining honest and committed to my relationship, but I somehow managed to keep my sanity intact.

My time at Big FM was hardly easy. Every day was a test of talent and patience. There was a lot of pressure, especially with seniors raving, ranting, standing on my head while I doled out live on-air links. There was no scope for mistakes. Luckily, I made friends with my producers, who made my life easy. Earlier on, it was Shruti and later Rani, who has always been this amazing super woman.

Rani is this extraordinarily efficient professional who I became so comfortable working with that her being in the studio with me while I conducted my show didn't bother me at all. In fact, she was well-versed with Delhi and would often give me material for the show. Since I hadn't lived in Delhi before, my knowledge of the city was limited, but she knew exactly which flyover was where, where you'd find the best buy for your living room carpet, where you'd find paranthas at 2 a.m., which were the best places to hang out, the best moongfaliwalla in the city, and so on.

She knew just about everything and we made a formidable team. In fact, that was the time she told me that someday I would be a star and she would manage my career. I laughed it off then. (A small note here: nine years later, now in 2015, Rani does manage me though I don't know how much of a star

I am. This was after she had dabbled with many jobs in Dubai and it almost seemed like she would never come back to India. And I was still struggling with my career.

During my radio days in Delhi, I was staying with my maternal aunt, Sunita Maasi, who has been working as a librarian at Indian Institute of Public Administration, where all IAS officers work, and my uncle, her husband, who is a doctor. I was sharing the room with Siddharth, their son, who at that time was studying at St. Stephen's College, and had introduced me to something called Metallica. I was extremely happy, not just because of the job at Big FM, but because I was now a part of this big city. The fact that I was in Delhi and making a living for myself made me feel pretty content.

Everyone had their own life in the household I was staying in, but somehow, my uncle doubted my character. He couldn't fathom why I had chosen to work in radio; in his eyes it was a frivolous job to begin with, and was demanding so much of my time, at times even sixteen hours in a day. He formed his own conclusions and was convinced that I was goofing around, or to put it exactly the way he thought, sleeping around with girls. I don't know if he is still convinced about the pressures of my job. With the kind of work pressure at Big FM, forget about wooing and sleeping around with women, I think even married people didn't get much action with their better halves. Both my aunt and uncle loved me, but my uncle still switched on the television in the room where I slept to watch the news of 6 a.m., despite me having reached home at 3 a.m.

That was the time I decided to shift out to a rented apartment; I deserved some rest after a tiring day at work. This new development wasn't essentially liberating, as running a household was not my cup of tea. My mom had to come down from Chandigarh every weekend to ensure that the house was in order. I mostly lived at work; so much so that Rani found me a corner in the office where I slept for two hours every day.

Amongst my close friends there were Manisha, Shruti, Rani, Manish Gunthey and Pavan Sharma. Praveen, our marketing head, was really sweet. Her daughter was my fan. Surprising as it might sound, as an RJ, I too had fans, though I am not sure how loyal they were. Most of them, I realized over a period of time, were 'anoraks'; basically those who are addicted to the radio and frequently call up all the RJs at all the stations. Perhaps it was the new wave of viewer appeasement that attracted listeners in hordes. Every show had a contest and some prize attached to it. So I wasn't really sure if the listeners were fans of our voices and content or followed us for the prizes.

But there was one person who truly was my fan. His name was Divender Sharma and he lived in a place called Bagpat, which is close to Delhi. He used to religiously listen to my show every morning while on the train to Delhi on his way to work. On weekends, he used to specially come to office with half a kilo of balushai, an Indian sweet, which had precisely eight pieces. And there was always only one piece left for me. The rest was polished off by Rani, Manish and the others. Actually, they knew that if the dabba reached me, I would devour all of it by myself, like I had done on several other occasions.

So as a rule, the box always reached me last, with only piece left in it. It was the most amazing balushai I have ever had. Once, an idea struck me, and I began expressing my foodie desires on air in the hope that some or the other loyal fan might find a culinary way to impress me. And it worked!

Shruti used to bring dahi ki sabzi to the office, which I loved. Recently when I went to Delhi's Red

FM office to promote 'Mitti di Khushboo', Shruti got me the same delicious sabzi. I was touched by her sweet gesture. From being a trainee working under me to being the programme head at Red FM today, she has come a long way. She makes me proud.

I remember this funny incident around Valentine's Day when we ran a contest in which the winner would get to go on a date with me. So here I had an official chance to date a hot woman, but sadly all the hot ones were not giving the right answers. Shruti selected a winner, overlooking all the hot ones! Though personally disappointed, I think I somehow managed to impress the winner.

■

The drill at Big FM continued for another two years, and like I said before, it drained the life out of me. Even though it was increasingly becoming a struggle for me to drag myself to office, trust me, I gave my hundred per cent each day. This was when I knew that it was time for me to take that leap of faith: go back to Mumbai to do what I always dreamed of doing—becoming an actor. No one took me seriously in office, but since they knew I was confident, they supported my decision. They even offered me the option of conducting shows from the Mumbai office. In fact, they were generous enough to let me use the Big FM accommodation in Mumbai. Kind though they were, I did get to know something from my previous producer, Shruti, about what had happened behind closed doors during this time. Remember I told you earlier about the time Tarun said that he'll make sure I become an actor when I expressed my aspirations for the same in front of him? When I knew I had to go to Mumbai and they were being all kind to me, little did I know that they didn't have faith in me at all. Shruti told me that Tarun had said, 'Jane do isko, do hafte main waapis aayega.'

(With God's grace, it's been over seven years and I still haven't gone back!)

Gradually, I started auditioning in Mumbai, while giving links for Big FM Delhi. At no point of my life did I put myself in a situation where I was cash-strapped. I never put all my eggs in one basket. I didn't want to leave Big FM till the time I had something concrete on the acting front. And I think even they didn't want me to go because I was doing a good job. Soon, my first Balaji serial happened—*Qayamat*, where I played the second lead. And my not-so-memorable stint in television fiction shows started.

■

During my stint with Big FM, apart from running my show, I also interviewed celebrities who would drop by to promote their movies or a cause. I remember my first celebrity interview was with Abhishek Bachchan, who came on the show to promote his film, *Guru*. Saying that I was nervous would be an understatement. I sat in front of him and asked routine questions, recording the interview on this humble flash recorder that I used to carry everywhere. When you are nervous, you don't really try and be funny or witty or entertaining. And if you try, you'll most probably end up making a fool of yourself. Hence, I stuck to routine.

Another interesting interview was with actress Kim Sharma, who at that time was apparently dating cricketer Yuvraj Singh. It was a janta interview—basically, she was addressing a whole bunch of journos, a miniscule part of which I was. Since Sudha my programming head, was aggressive about getting content, she pushed me to ask Kim a controversial question. And there, amidst the cacophony of journalists, came my timid question that immediately resonated in the mall where we were interviewing her.

I'm sure most of you are familiar with those

moments in life where you assume that your voice will drown in the sea of noise and you'll get away with it, but apparently what happens is just the opposite. The moment you open your mouth and those words that you never meant to utter come popping out, and there is this eerie silence that does nothing more than establish the audacity of your stupid question.

That is exactly what happened to me. I had the balls to ask her about Yuvraj, and suddenly there was this awkward silence in which she just stared at me with a blank expression. Her and everyone else's eyes were on me and I just wanted to bury my head somewhere, like an ostrich. Fortunately, Manish came to the rescue, quickly established that it was rather a stupid question and that everyone should continue with the interview, and whisked me away.

That wasn't the only time I made a fool of myself; the examples are bountiful. Out of them, one more that I still remember vividly is the one where I had to interview Shahrukh Khan. I had just shifted to Mumbai and was still recording links for Big FM. It was a huge moment for me for I have been his fan ever since I can remember. He was shooting for an ad for Hyundai at Hiranandani (Powai) and I was anxiously waiting outside his vanity van to interview him. Just the fact that I was breathing in the same air as him was enough to give me a high. I stole a few glances of him shooting and even though I waited for four hours outside his vanity, I didn't complain one bit; they seemed like fleeting moments. Sitting there, I wrote the world's most embarrassing letter.

It went something like this:

Dear Shahrukh sir,

I am a huge fan of yours, and I am the same guy in blue shorts you met in Kasauli in 1995 while you were there shooting for *Maya Memsaab*. You, I remember, were wearing a red suit. Now that same boy has grown up to become an RJ and wants to be an actor. Please give me a chance to prove myself. I'll be very grateful.

Yours sincerely,
Ayushmann.

Even reminiscing about what I had written gives me the creeps, though it also makes me crack up at my juvenile self. I know what you are wondering: did I give that letter to him or not? And if I did, what was his response? I think I read that letter at least a hundred times. Finally, I realized that it was the lamest thing ever. Slipping the letter into my pocket, I got up and left. Yes, I came back without giving the letter or taking the interview. Like I said, just watching him made me happy.

Another embarrassing instance was my interview with filmmaker Karan Johar. As I've mentioned earlier, I was in Mumbai working for radio where the Indian Television Academy Awards were being held. I was hoping that my name would be suggested by Big FM for hosting the red carpet, as they were supposed to give the names of two radio jockeys for the same. The red carpet event was being televised.

Unfortunately, Tarun didn't forward my name; instead Archana Jani and Rohit got to host the red carpet. I was a little envious as I was pushed inside a booth where I had to interview celebs and it was being aired on all forty-five stations of Big FM. But as luck would have it, amongst the many celebs who came to the booth was Karan Johar. In between the interview, I expressed my desire to become an actor and asked for his phone number.

His priceless expression clearly said: 'Really? You expect me to give you my personal number and that too on air so that the rest of the country also knows it?!' I understood and quickly told him that he could give me his number post the interview—as if I was obliging him! At the end of the interview, he gave me his office landline number.

I was extremely excited and thought to myself, 'Ab toh life set hai. Ab mujhe koi rok nahin sakta! Ab toh introducing Ayushmann Khurrana hai by Dharma Productions!' The next day I dialled the number Karan had given me. They said Karan wasn't in office. The day after that, I called again and they said he was busy. And, finally, my bubble burst when, the subsequent day, they told me bluntly, 'We only work with stars, and can't work with you.'

Ouch. That hurt. But I don't blame them. Now that I think about it, just how many people must be calling them each day, every minute? Which is what leads me to my next code. But before that, another humiliating experience—one that happened after I was told that I must do some lobbying to get work.

I was in touch with this gentleman called Anurag Rao, who was essentially an event manager, but also managed actors—he was Neha Dhupia's manager at that time. We met a couple of times and he then invited me to a 'Page 3' party, suggesting that I build contacts there. When I reached the swanky hotel where the party was, I saw fancy cars lined up, causing me to park my humble car somewhere down the lane in an effort to hide it from view. So you see, my pretense started then only.

As I entered the room, my eyes popped out as I saw the entire Bollywood fraternity there. There was Karan Johar, Sohail Khan, Salman Khan, Shilpa Shetty; every celeb you could think of was in attendance. Assuming I would make solid contacts and friends for life here, I entered the place with a confident stride. But, sadly, nobody even acknowledged my royal presence, let alone bother striking a conversation with me.

I felt so out of place. The only person who spoke to me was Rahul Khanna, who complimented me on the way I had hosted 'I Am She', the Miss Universe beauty pageant. But other than that, nothing. Now, I could have either hung around at that party like a loser for another two hours or quietly made my exit. Thankfully, I chose the latter. That night was an eye-opener for me. The elite world that I aspired to enter had depressed me—not because I wasn't a part of it, but because I was being forced to be a part of it in order to become an actor.

Code #6: *There is no point in being one of many; no point in running towards fame; absolutely no point in doing PR; no point in being ordinary. You have to rise above the rest in your given circumstances. Only then will people take notice of you. I ran around and after. I am confessing that I did. This code can perhaps save you from the embarrassing moments that I went through. Hold your ground. Let your talent, your work, speak for you. There is not a chance you'll be missed if you strive for excellence.*

6

The 'I' of the Idiot Box

YOU REMEMBER I had told you about the TV serial that I was part of? So here, at *Qayamat*, a Balaji serial that ran on Star Plus, I was playing the second lead who was mostly a part of passing shots and silent expressions. My first shot was to behave clumsily and fall; it reminded me of my first ever play. I knew I didn't want to do this for long. A new channel called Zee Next was being launched and I got the lead in one of the serials, *Ek Thi Rajkumari,* opposite Neha Marda.

Joining the new show was fun but leaving *Qayamat* was painful; not for me, but for the producers. I remember the Balaji team kept pestering me to sign their contract if I wanted my payment of ₹1.5 lakh, which was due to me. I kept procrastinating. They threatened me that if I didn't sign, I would never get the money. The contract said I would be bound to them for the next three years.

At that time, money meant a lot and I needed it too, but I didn't succumb to the temptation. When I left without signing the contract, I got to know that Ekta threw a fit and smashed her mobile by hurling it at the executive producer's face.

Just an afterthought: last year, there were talks of me acting in *Milan Talkies*, being produced by Ekta Kapoor, though the project got shelved later. This leads me to another quintessential code, the one that I hear from my father-in-law quite often, and the one that I have now experienced way too often.

Code #7: *There are no permanent friends or permanent foes, only permanent interests.*

Anyway, I wasn't let go on a happy note. Since I hadn't signed the contract, there was no legal action they could have taken, but the number of threatening calls and messages I received from them were quite intimidating. I was told that my career was finished, that I should not stay in Mumbai and simply pack my bags and go back to Chandigarh. I didn't let that affect me much, even though I knew that there was nobody in Mumbai who could have protected me if the need had arisen.

I knew there was nothing wrong in what I had done, and letting go of the show was necessary for my career. Soon *Ek Thi Rajkumari* was happening, where I was playing the negative lead. Big FM was there, too, but films weren't happening. I had made peace with the television world at that point of time. I thought that perhaps this was my fate and I'd just hop from one TV show to another, and that would be my life.

The fact is that TV actors are paid handsomely; at times even better than many Bollywood actors. I wouldn't have been an unhappy wreck if (God forbid) films hadn't happened. But my dream had always been to make it to Bollywood—to sing, dance, romance, fight and pack in lots of drama. I used to sit in the small balcony of my modest Malad West flat, where I used to look across the street at a huge hoarding with posters of the latest films splashed flamboyantly. I always nurtured the dream to have my film's hoarding displayed there. But life was stagnant at that time and I thought films just might never happen. I had made my peace with it, and was still happy and grateful. Then one day I got a call from Nirupam, Raghu's friend. He told me that MTV was auditioning for fresh faces for a show called *Wassup,* and I had been referred by my friend, Gaurav Kapoor.

Quick flashback: Gaurav had been a trainer at MICA around two-and-a-half years ago. I didn't know I had left an impression on him.

> **Code #8:** *Give your best to whatever opportunity you get; never underestimate the significance of even the smallest of junctures. Your past actions will one day become your future redemption.*

I was thrilled to bits on hearing the news, and went for the audition. I remember José and Bani queued up for the audition as well. We went through numerous rounds, and I MADE it! The salary was half of what I was making from my television shows, but that didn't matter. I just knew that if I made it as a VJ, then films wouldn't be a distant dream. That day was the happiest day of my life.

It was the first time I stood in my balcony crying while looking at the hoarding. My dreams now seemed achievable. I have never cried; success or failure doesn't affect me much, as I know it's going to be temporary, but that day was very special. It is something I can't express through words.

Thus began the time when I was working three jobs simultaneously—*Ek Thi Rajkumari*, Big FM and MTV's *Wassup*. I worked for around twenty hours every day and slept only in the car on my way from one shoot to the other. And this is also the time when my radio show became the number one show in Delhi. Gradually, I left Big FM and then, eventually, the TV serial. After that, I was just doing MTV. The best times of my life—both professionally and personally—happened was while I was working with MTV.

In retrospect, there is one thing that has remained constant over the years: whichever job I took, I have left it only after giving it my best—except for *Qayamat* which I don't consider a job but more of an experience. I joined Big FM and left it when my show became number one; *Ek Thi Rajkumari* when it became one of the highest rated shows on Zee Next; MTV, when I learned how not to be a wannabe and when my show, *Fantastic Five,* got good ratings; *India's Got Talent* (IGT) after I did two successful seasons; *Music Ka Maha Muqqabla* after Season 1 of IGT; and then *Just Dance,* with which I became the highest paid non-celeb host on Indian television.

Mind you, this is not about going on an ego trip

or boasting about what I've done. It's about a code that I wish to share with you:

> **Code #9:** *Aspire for the next thing when you think you deserve it. Once you have proved yourself worthy of the current situation and have become big for it, only then try outgrowing it by venturing to the next level. It's part of a progressive growth ladder, and also a predecessor to a success story.*

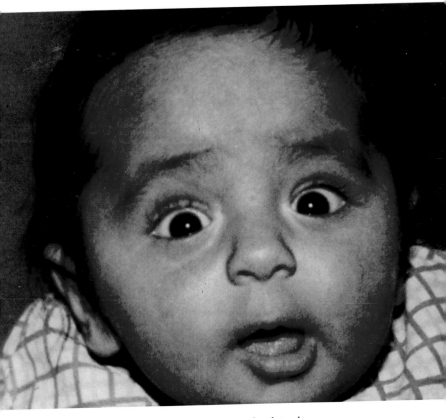

Clearly surprised at being born.

Trying to look as pretty as a girl.

With mom and dad.

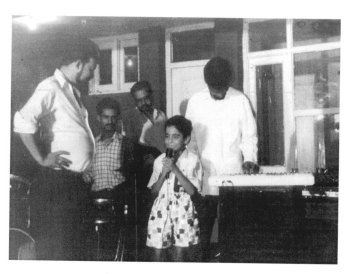

The stage has always allured me.

Fashion conscious (remember, being presentable was the only option I had).

My trademark 'joota hai japani' act.

The gawky teenage years.

On the sets of **Madras Cafe** *with John Abraham.*

Behind the scenes of Bewakoofiyaan.

On the sets of Nautanki Saala.

During the making of 'Paani da rang'.

7

VJ Ayushmann

AS A ROOKIE VJ, I wasn't treated or accepted like one initially. I remember how difficult it was in the beginning. When we were shooting for the pilot of *Wassup*, we had to cover an autorickshaw race at Hiranandani with Smriti as a producer (today, she works with Saif Ali Khan's production house, Illuminati Films.) I was so bad at it, however, that the episode was never aired.

The struggle didn't end there. The first time I shot for *Wassup* inside the studio, I couldn't even read my lines properly on the teleprompter. This made Tanvi Gandhi, the producer of the show, extremely nervous. I'm sure she must have thought that I would end up jeopardizing her career. Thankfully, she's doing extremely well for herself today, working with Anurag Kashyap on his most ambitious film yet, *Bombay Velvet*.

Anyway, it's clear that I was a big disaster in the beginning at MTV. I was always nervous. It took time and effort from both MTV and myself to warm up to each other. And, thankfully, after two or three episodes, people started liking me. After this I began to get maximum time as a studio anchor. Thereon, the ratings also climbed. Also, during my teething phase at MTV, there were a lot of people who had a problem with me starting my show with 'Namaskar' and signing off with 'Ayushmannbhava'. It was considered uncool.

Then came the day when Nikhil Chinappa wasn't available, and I had to fill in for him at *MTV Select*. The moment was surreal for me because I had grown up watching the show. But later I was snubbed because I had hosted the show in Hindi. Instead of getting bogged down and becoming bitter about the second-hand treatment being meted out to a Hindi-speaking VJ, I decided to acknowledge that perhaps something in me was amiss.

So I started observing and absorbing even more. I started writing Hinglish scripts, since it took me time to convert my thoughts into English before saying them out loud. This transition happened organically.

Slowly, the conversion time reduced and, eventually, English started flowing naturally...and when it did, MTV became a Hindi-language channel! Talk about timing!

In retrospect, had I not seen this humiliating phase at MTV, I would have never evolved from being a small-town Hindi-speaking boy. Though I believe that, deep down, I am still the same, I have learned to be a part of the cool crowd over time. Finally!

Besides the many problems I faced, I also noticed that, for the first six months at MTV, my profile wasn't put up on the channel website. Bani, José and everyone else were featured but not me. It still remains a mystery to me. I must confess that I used to be quite a nerd, or 'uncool' as they say it, when it came to clothes—pointed shoes, loose trousers, spectacles... basically, a disaster. My styling gradually changed by observing the uber chic crowd around me.

There is this incident I remember that was most humiliating for me. I have never felt so low and small in my entire life; never have I been abused as much. This was a press conference I had to host at the uber posh Taj Lands End for the movie *Ghajini*. It went badly because it was my first, and I messed up the sequence. Sameer Chopra from the Viacom team abused the hell out of me. I apologized endlessly, but he just didn't stop. He didn't spare me at all. Since I had recently got married, I was really scared about my future.

Then there was another press conference for *Roadies* Season 5, again at the Taj Lands End, and that too didn't go well. The jinx with this hotel was finally broken when I hosted my best ever press conference for *Just Dance*.

■

At MTV, I started acting in spoofs like 'Cheque de India' and 'Jaddu Jaddu Ek Ek Baar Baar'. And for the first time here, I got genuine appreciation. I got to travel a lot as a VJ and hosted many shows, including ones at IIM Ahmedabad, Lucknow and Kashipur. In fact, at IIM Ahmedabad I was felicitated as a celeb host. Interestingly, it is this institute that I had aspired to be a part of at one point. Yes, I had taken MBA classes, too!

Then I got a show called *Fantastic Five*. It was an interesting show during which I used to write my own scripts. No other VJ did that. I knew that I didn't have the gift of gab yet, so I rehearsed a lot. Rajesh Narsimhan (now with Yash Raj Films), deputy to Ashish Patil (now the head of Yash Raj Talent

Management and Y Films) was amazed by my notes. Both of us have grown together from MTV to YRF.

I remember not being given a vanity van while shooting for 'Cheque De India'. I slept where the artists' clothes used to be ironed. Cyrus Sahukar was shocked to see this. He asked me to demand a van, as it was every artist's right. And when I asked for one, I got it. It was just that I had never demanded one.

Another interesting anecdote I vividly remember was with our DOP, Akshay Rajput. One day I said to him, 'Sir, main actor banna chahta hoon. Mujhe loge kabhie?' Pat came his reply, 'Main Rannvijay ko loonga, tereko nahi loonga.' Needless to say, I felt bad, because he was an amazing DOP. It's human nature to feel bad if you fall low in someone's estimation, especially someone you really look up to.

Before *Vicky Donor*'s release, Akshay had told a friend of mine, Vineet Modi, who was the photographer for the *Roadies* season that went to Brazil: 'Mujhe nahin lagta Ayush kuch kar payega. He doesn't have the spark.' Well, that is that. I am happy where I am today and still have tremendous respect for Akshay.

> **Code #10:** *Critics are your best friends. They bring out the best in you. Never shun them, criticize them or run them down. They have an opinion because of some reason. That reason will eventually be the reason for your growth.*

During the time I was hosting shows at MTV, I signed up for this movie that not many know of. It was an embarrassing oversight, and I thank the forces above for pulling me out of it at the right time. The movie was called...believe it or not...*KLPD*.

Yeah, now you can shut that open jaw. That was precisely my wife's reaction when I told her the full-form of this term. Well, the second meaning that was bestowed upon this abbreviation by the writer and director Annirudh Chawla was 'Kisses, Love, Pyar and Dosti'. This guy worked with Big FM and had offered me this script. The script was useless and didn't make sense to me but I was really desperate to do a movie, and my wife understood my desperation.

Armed with her consent, I ventured to Bangkok for an indefinite time with Yash Tonk and Kushal Punjabi who were the other leads, along with the three girls paired opposite us. Later, this movie, obviously sans me, was released as *Balls Hai Kya?* and, as expected, bombed at the box office and went unnoticed. My eviction from this project was a blessing in disguise and, for this reason, I truly believe in this one thing, the baap of all codes: destiny.

Had *KLPD* been part of my destiny, I don't know where I would have been—certainly not in a position to write this book! I discussed this project with Ashish Patil, the CEO of MTV. He told me not to do it and said it was absolute bullshit. But then, kaun samajhata mujhe? I desperately wanted to act in a movie. So I went ahead with it. We reached Bangkok and began to workout everyday on the beach.

Strangely, the producer was extremely generous with the finances. He was spending money left, right and centre. In fact, I have to admit that I shopped there and it was all on the house. Obviously, I offered to pay but he dismissed my offer, saying that we would look into it later. A hilarious incident occurred one day when we were running on the beach and we saw some girls running behind us. Instant ego high! But as they approached us, instead of stopping and flirting with them, we sprinted even faster as we realized that they were lady boys!

Amidst all this, only one thing wasn't happening—the film shoot that we had come here for. It had been nearly five days since this routine of eating, sleeping and working out had begun, and the shoot still hadn't started. Thankfully, I was called back by MTV. To tell you the truth, I was the only one who managed to leave that place unscathed. A few more days in Bangkok, and I would have been stuck there, just like the rest of them, without work or money. Yes, the entire cast and crew were detained. It so happened that the producers of the film kept procrastinating about their payments, that never came. Sunny Narula, the guy who was in charge of the finances, was apparently under huge debt. The local 'Sardar', or manager, in Bangkok happened to be a don. He confiscated everyone's passports and threatened to hold them until the money came in. Sunny, being confident about his ability to repay the money, had given the passports to the don. And that was it. The money didn't come and everyone went through a hellish experience for a month, without money and without anything to do.

Kushal and Yash, I believe, somehow managed to come back to India after a few days of living through the hell. But for the rest, I heard it was like an endless nightmare. It could have been me, too, but thank God for small mercies.

8

The New 'Anchor' of the Reality Ship

NON-FICTION SHOWS WERE coming up in a big way, in the meantime. And I think I was one of the first MTV VJ to do both MTV and host non-fiction reality shows on General Entertainment Channels. There was a time when I was offered *India's Got Talent* and the *Indian Premiere League* (IPL) to host at the same time. I really wanted to do *India's Got Talent*, but they said that they wouldn't give me money as MTV and Colours were sister concerns and both come under the Viacom 18 umbrella.

For once, I was sure that I was not going to be taken for granted. Talks were on with IPL, who readily agreed to pay me much more than what MTV had pitched for me. I hosted the IPL and then, on the basis of that, pitched for *India's Got Talent* and finally got separate remuneration for it. I am very bad with finances and numbers, but not at the cost of being taken for a ride. It pays to be aware of what the norms are in the business one is in.

IPL was a learning experience, no doubt, but not the most enjoyable one. It was live and there was no scope for even a small error. There was way too much pressure than what I had bargained for. And *India's Got Talent* was just the diametric opposite. I had the time of my life there, besides experiencing one of the biggest learning lessons of my life.

It all started with the auditions. I did what I could and I guess it was very well received. I used to write my own script, entertain everyone with my one-liners, and generally did my own improvisations without depending too much on the teleprompter. By the end of the audition rounds, I realized that I was the only constant while the other anchors were being rotated and paired alongside me. I was still not one hundred per cent certain that I had made it. RJs, VJs and other television hosts were tried with me as my co-hosts. Hiten Tejwani, Nikhil Chinnappa, Cyrus Sahukar, and a host of others joined in. Finally, Nikhil and I were confirmed. I felt proud to be working for

Siddarth Basu's company. *India's Got Talent* started, and I had a great time travelling the length and breadth of the country with Nikhil. Amongst the many other things that I have to credit him with, there is one life-altering moment that happened for which I am extremely grateful to him—flying business class! Nikhil always travelled business during MTV, so obviously it was his prerequisite at IGT, too, and because they couldn't make him travel economy, I got to travel business for the first time! It was a big achievement for me.

Nikhil is this extremely intelligent person; he is full of knowledge, worldly wisdom and experience. I knew I could learn a lot from him. He taught me the smallest of things like the art of tipping, gentlemen's etiquette and appreciating different cultures, to life lessons in general. On IGT, I perhaps had a slight edge over him because of my fluency in Hindi. But, in life, I still have a lot to learn from him, which is why, every year, Teacher's Day begins with me wishing him.

That season of IGT with Kirron Kher, Shekhar Kapur and Sonali Bendre was the best one for me. We all shared great camaraderie. It was a balancing act between Nikhil and me. He predominantly gave links in English while my Hindi made me connect with the masses. In fact, I think Kirron Kher enjoyed my inherent 'Punjabi' sense of humour the most. Life looked good for me again, as there was a beautiful harmony that existed between home and the world outside.

Soon, I got a chance to host a show solo for the first time—*Music Ka Maha Muqqabla*. I would like to take this platform to admit that it was a terrible experience for me. I was always nervous on the set because things were perpetually mismanaged and disorganized. That's also when I came to know that a lot of things are predetermined in reality shows. The judges are at the beck and call of the channel. Somebody deserves to win but someone else does. For the greed of TRPs, channels introduce their own twists and turns. Sometimes, though not always, the judges' decision is diluted because of the channel's say-so. The channel always has the last word.

The judges on the show were Shaan, Mika, Mohit Chauhan, Shankar Mahadevan and Himesh Reshammiya. The most revered amongst them was Shankar and the most controversial were Himesh and Mika. They were, in fact, instructed by the channel to speak their mind without thinking twice. Basically, they were asked to blurt out anything that would help the show grab eyeballs and, subsequently, TRPs.

Later, I was offered the third season of IGT after having delivered two successful seasons. At the same time, however, also I got an offer from *Just Dance*. I had to pick one and was in two minds. The dilemma was to either ride high on the successful franchise of IGT, something that was well within my comfort zone, or be a part of a much bigger show, *Just Dance*, which was being projected as Hrithik's show. I wanted to do IGT but *Just Dance* was a bigger opportunity.

I did realize there was a possibility of getting completely ignored on the show because of Hrithik's presence and his image of being the God of dance that was being promoted as the USP of the show. I knew very well that if I was to do the show, I had to carve out my own identity by being bloody good at my job. The few inhibitions that remained in me were put to rest when I went to host Star Parivar Awards in Macau. That's where I had a meeting with Star TV honchos and I laid down two conditions—first, that I be a solo host, and second, that I be paid an obnoxious amount yet unheard of! I thought they wouldn't agree and I'd soon be back on IGT (as I've mentioned earlier, back then, nobody earned that much as a non-celeb host on television).

Fortunately or unfortunately, both my conditions were agreed to and with that I became the anchor of the show, *Just Dance*. This was a turning point for me. For the first time, I felt like a celeb myself when I travelled to different cities for the auditions with Farah Khan and Vaibhavi Merchant, who were there as judges. My entry was marked with cheers and whistles. People started recognizing me and I used to feed off their energies.

I was becoming more confident, more in control of my craft by the minute. The auditions happened in Delhi, Calcutta, Mumbai and New York. This was the first time an Indian reality show was going international, and was being made on such a huge budget. New York was so much fun. I was shooting at the Times Square and Statue of Liberty—exotic locations I'd only heard of before.

The auditions happening at Manhattan had the Indian diaspora from across North America in attendance. There was a flood of Gujaratis, Punjabis and Pakistanis as well. What surprised me the most was that the crowd knew my name. Here, I realized that my experience at MTV had helped me prepare fun content for anchoring, which set me apart from the other 'Hello friends' anchors.

The auditions became a bonding ground for the judges and me. We partied together, and became good friends later on. There were initial hiccups, but post the first five episodes, I was on the right track and had begun enjoying my work.

> **Code #11:** *Sometimes you have to make a choice that you may not be comfortable with initially. You have to make a conscious effort to push yourself to avoid becoming stagnant. I could have easily chosen* India's Got Talent *Season 3 as it was completely in my comfort zone. It was home to me but it was time to move ahead.*

At *Just Dance,* another point worth mentioning is that there were three judges, thousands of participants, but only one anchor. I knew I had to make the most of it.

This was also the time when the exaggerated nature of reality TV shows first hit me. Every time some contestant won the round, they were applauded and encouraged as if they would be the next big thing in Bollywood. For instance, Ankan, a contestant who won the show, and another participant, Karan Khanna, who came third, were given such praise and shown so many false dreams that they must have thought they have made already it big. I had learnt this lesson from my stint at *Popstars* and, thankfully, post MTV *Roadies*, I wasn't disillusioned.

But these kids were being told time and again that they were future superstars. I knew that after a year no one would remember who Ankan or Karan Khanna were, but they were given false hopes and were promised a fantasy world in which fans mobbed them to take their autographs and photographs. This was perhaps to get the best or worst out of them, probably for the sake of the TRPs. I really don't know the reason, but I could see a young me in them and yet couldn't tell them what I felt or knew.

Maybe this platform will help me convey this to the thousands of aspirants of reality shows: remember, there are seasons after seasons of a particular show. Two to three reality shows run on every channel at any given point of time. Meanwhile, there are as many shows running on other channels, too. Then again there are at least eight to ten entertainment channels. This is not to dissuade anyone from trying their luck, of course. But if you think you are the only one, then this is just a gentle reminder: there are many who have been there and many who will be and still many who will simultaneously share your moment of glory on some other channel.

Public attention is fickle. Today, they like you because you are on-screen perhaps doing what they would like to see you do. Tomorrow is going to be another season. Another set of new contestants. Another disillusioned winner. You need to figure out what you are. You just can't be a reality show winner all your life.

Forget the winners; even the participants begin to think that they have already achieved big success, and many of them immediately shift base to Mumbai and get lost in the crowd. They don't realize that they were just characters who suited the flavour of the season at that particular time. Tell me honestly, after Season 2 of *Roadies*, do you think I could have been selected for any other season? Obviously not! I just happened to suit a prerequisite that the creators of the show had in mind during that season and that's that. In the forthcoming seasons, the format changed and so did the requirements. That's when the reality of the situation dawned on me. I knew that only being a *Roadies* winner would not make me an actor. After reading so far, you as the reader already know the kind of struggle that lay ahead. I am reiterating this fact at the risk of sounding preachy, but being a reality show winner will not help you become an actor!

Looking at a few of the *Just Dance* contenders, Rajat Dev, who came fourth, is still doing what he was doing before getting selected for the show. Ankan is still assisting someone. Karan Khanna is not doing anything in this field at all. Surjit sirji opened a dance institute in Delhi, though I don't know how it is faring today. Forget about becoming stars; most of them are just doing what they were doing before they came on the show.

In fact, the TV channel benefits more than any of these participants do individually. How somebody chooses to utilize their moment of glory also depends on their own drive. Either this success on a reality show could mean everything for the person or they could treat it like a means to an end.

Personally, I think I benefitted the most from *Just Dance*. With this show, I got really popular and not only bagged an award for best anchor, but also earned a newfound respect in the film fraternity, which actually meant the most to me. This was a life-altering show for me, as this is where Shoojit Sircar noticed me and approached me for the lead role in my acting debut, *Vicky Donor*.

Code #12: *It may be an overused and abused maxim, but it becomes life-altering if paid heed to: 'Wisdom lies in learning from others' experiences.'*

I have known it to be true and am therefore sharing the same with you. Become more than just a reality show contestant or winner. It's only then that you are truly noticed.

9

Ticket to Bollywood

VICKY DONOR WAS my ticket to tinsel town. As I have
mentioned before, my work on *Just Dance* got me
noticed by Shoojit Sircar. I didn't have to audition
for this role; the script just fell into my lap. Not
that I was their first choice—Vivek Oberoi wanted to
produce and act in *Vicky Donor*, and they had almost
signed him up, but for some reason Ronnie Screwvala,
the producer, changed his mind. The role was then
offered to Sharman Joshi, who politely declined it.
That's when the film came to me.

I think my image really helped them make this
choice. Since the topic was a bit edgy, they needed an
endearing character. I got a call from Jogi, the casting
director, as he had earlier auditioned me for a movie

called *Teen The Bhai*. Trust me when I say that I had killed that audition. I am usually over critical of myself but I know when I am really good at an audition. They took five more auditions, but eventually I wasn't selected for Mrigdeep Singh Lamba's directorial debut.

At that time, I didn't know why I hadn't been chosen for *Teen The Bhai*. But in retrospect, it's good that I wasn't, as there was something far better waiting for me. But who could explain this to me at that point of time! I was so depressed that, for the first time, I carried the disappointment home with me, making Tahira sad too. I was upset because I thought the movie would have been perfect for me. Rakesh Omprakash Mehra was producing the film about three Punjabi brothers. Eventually, they chose Shreyas Talpade over me. The good that came from that audition was that it made Jogi Paaji; as I fondly call him notice me; he made a mental note of my performance, which is why he gave me a chance with *Vicky Donor*.

Another rejection came in the form of *I Hate Love Stories* where Imran Khan and Sonam Kapoor were to play the leads. Here I was, with a heavy heart, auditioning for the role of a side character in this movie. And I was rejected even for that! You can never assume what life has in store for you. Who had known life would come full circle when, a couple of years down the line, I would be paired opposite Sonam in *Bewakoofiyaan*!

> **Code #13:** Sometimes you don't get an opportunity as there is a better one waiting for you. This might sound bookish and idealistic but if *Teen The Bhai* or *I Hate Love Stories* had happened, *Vicky Donor* would have never happened, and this code wouldn't have been typed out.

Another memorable audition that I remember was for *Bhaag Milkha Bhaag*. I grew my beard and tied a turban on my head, locked myself in a room, and recorded the audition on my handycam. I think Tahira wondered if I had really lost it by then. But she's always given me space without being judgmental or even being vocal about her concerns.

I did get a call post the audition telling me that Rakeshji had liked it. But as fate would have it, Farhan got it and did complete justice to the role of The Flying Sikh, Milkha Singh.

Coming back to *Vicky Donor*, a meeting was finally arranged between Shoojit da and me. This is how it went: He said 'Kaisa hai tu, theek hai? Sperm donor ka movie hai, karega?' I was shocked. He gave me

the script and said, 'Padhke bata kaisa laga tereko.'
I read it and really liked it, as it was an interesting
subject and the script was really good. He then asked,
'Karega?' I said, 'Haan, karega.' Who was I to say no
to a filmmaker of Shoojit da's stature!

Like I said, Sharman Joshi had refused to play
Vicky. In fact, Vinay Pathak, Boman Irani and Om
Puri were offered the role eventually portrayed by
Anu Kapoor, which they all refused. Anuji later got
a National Award for that role.

Throughout the making of *Vicky Donor*, I was more
or less numb, lost and quite underconfident. I didn't
know what was happening around me. I just did what
Shoojit da asked me to do. And if I ever wanted to
give another take just to be sure, he wouldn't let me.
According to him, I was my most natural in the first
two takes, and if he took any more, then I would
start 'acting'.

I was nobody to doubt his craft or style of working.
But I didn't know how I looked onscreen or whether
my dialogue delivery was good or if I was doing justice
to the character. All I knew was that, despite being
unsure about my acting, I was having fun on the set.
I think I was at my innocent best and simply wanted
to contribute towards making a good movie. I even

gave the character of 'Biji' some interesting Punjabi one-liners that were accepted and incorporated into the script.

One day, just out of the blue, I made Shoojit da listen to the song that I had composed in my college days 'Paani da rang', and he seemed to like it. Basically, everything was going right during the making of the movie and, of course, we realized right after the release that we had done a mighty good job. The response was tremendous and overwhelming, to say the least. As soon as *Vicky Donor* reached the theatres, I was bombarded with incessant phone calls, text messages, emails, tweets and Facebook posts, all congratulating me. I remember around two weeks into its release, my friends and I decided to watch it together; the best part was that we couldn't get tickets of the film at any of the suburban multiplexes in Mumbai, and we tried at nearly six or seven of them! That was a really big high for me.

But one thing that was at an all-time low was my personal life with my wife. Suddenly, I became everyone's property; I wasn't hers alone. From the shy boy-next-door Ayushmann Khurrana, I had transformed into 'Oye Vicky!' or 'Ae sperm donor!'. Since neither my wife nor I had been exposed to such a drastic change in our lives, she didn't know what was happening and neither did I. We were totally clueless about how to react or respond to my sudden fame.

I just went along with the flow instead of trying to control it, leaving Tahira behind. It was not a conscious decision to revel in the newfound glory. To be honest, I didn't even enjoy as much, because I knew I didn't have my wife along to share it with. I was as lost as a teenager buying his first packet of condoms at the chemist's.

In fact, I didn't even realize when, at the first public event we attended together, I accidentally let go of her hand as I was accosted by the press. After about twenty minutes of jostling into the flashing strobes did I realize that I was not holding the hand of the person I had come with. When I turned around frantically to look for her, I saw her standing just where I had left her, with tears welling up in her eyes. I felt so miserable. I just wasn't in control of my life.

And neither am I today. Of course, I am better at handling my life than I was back then. But at that time, despite the roaring success of the movie, I wasn't happy. Personally, I was suffering a lot. I just couldn't give time to or share my success with my wife or my newly-born son. It was a messed up phase for me. Even though our relationship of twelve years perhaps helped us sail through this phase, the disconnect existed, not just with Tahira but with myself, too.

I had always wanted to be an actor, but I'd never thought about the frills the job came with, and about how much they would affect my life directly. At that stage, one truly becomes a loner. This sentiment was confirmed by Mithun da on the sets of my forthcoming film, *Hawaizaada*, when he said, 'Kya mila mujhe superstar ban ke? Ab main zyaada kush hoon. I was a loner then but I am much more sorted and happy today.' He told me that he had discussed the same with Amitabh Bachchan once, who felt the same way. This, despite the fact that they were both superstars of the eighties. Mithun da also confessed that every Friday he would run a temperature because of the stress and pressure that the job brought him.

Post *Vicky Donor*, I made a conscious decision to not let go of the most beautiful part of my life. The one that gives me permanent happiness, the one that is intangible and the one that is unconditional. So, I have started making conscious efforts to meet my family more often, and I try to go see them in Chandigarh even if it's just for a day or, at times, only for a couple of hours in a month.

Even though I haven't reached formidable heights in my career as of now, and I know that I still have a long way to go, but in retrospect I feel that the best time of my life was when I was working with MTV and had got recently married. Tahira was working as a lecturer at a mass communication college. We used to visit the malls, watch all the movies together, shop, eat, go for occasional holidays, and the little fame I had was enough to make my wife proud of me and for me to be only hers. But then again, the present is what I always wanted and what I signed up for, albeit without knowing about its repercussions.

Today I make sure that Tahira reads all the scripts that come my way, and her opinion matters a lot to me. We had, in fact, discussed the script of *Vicky Donor* and had shared our reservations over the few scenes that made us uncomfortable. But she was supportive of me. It is a different story that when she actually saw the kissing scene on big screen, she threw a fit.

And as if that wasn't enough, my second film, *Nautanki Saala,* created another big stir in our lives. The irony is that she wants to support me, as she knows it's just an act being played out in front of an impatient crew and a worried producer. But the wife in her takes precedence while watching my films, and then logic takes a backseat and things go haywire. We are still trying to help each other out in dealing with this. Negotiations are still on!

.

While playing Vicky in *Vicky Donor*, I took real-life references by picking up some traits of my 'slightly' loud brother, Aparshakti, and a friend, Aviral, and incorporating them into Vicky's character. Thankfully, it worked out pretty well. Before shooting began, I was sent for a month-long workshop with the famous Panditji, a.k.a Professor N.K. Sharma in Delhi to train for the role of Vicky.

Like I mentioned before, I wasn't auditioned for this movie; I just had a basic screen test with the casting director, Jogi. Shoojit da had told him to rehearse the scenes with me. So when I began rehearsing, the TV anchor in me refused to let go. Jogi said, 'Anchoring kam kar', and actually complained to Shoojit da that I was still an anchor. And that's when they sent me and Yami, my co-star, to Delhi for a month to attend an acting workshop. However, I was more receptive towards the workshop than Yami was. She thought it was madness. Face distortion, breathing and voice control/modulation classes didn't make any sense to her. I came from a theatre background and was pretty much used to the drill. She found it crazy initially, but she was already an actor on television; it was me who needed the grooming.

Panditji is quite an endearing character himself. If he's happy with you he'll only slap you, and if not, then God save your ears from his chaste Hindi abuses. He is part of the NSD repertoire and runs a reputed theatre group called 'Act One' in Delhi. During the workshops, I worked a lot on my body language, and practised several improvisations that really helped us warm up for the shoot that followed. In short, and in no particular order, this was my journey of bringing to life the whack job who is now popular as *Vicky Donor*.

Then began a testing time in my life. It particularly wasn't a low period, but definitely a learning lesson. It was the time I had signed up for *Nautanki Saala*. I really thought it would do well, but that was right after signing the movie and reading the script. Initially there wasn't any script; it was still being written, although I had seen (and loved) the French film, *Après Vous*, from which it was being adapted.

I have always liked Rohan Sippy's work at large. His movies are big canvas portraits of life—be it *Dum Maro Dum* or even *Bluffmaster*. In the end, however, I felt disappointed I had presumed it was going to be something like his previous outings. Moreover, because I never understood numbers or budgets, I didn't look at the finer print. Later when I came to know that it was to be a small-budget movie, I felt somewhat let down.

I don't blame Rohan Sippy one bit, however. I guess his intentions were always clear. It was perhaps a miscommunication or something, but in my head I clearly hadn't signed up for what was coming my way. This happened after I was taken under the wings of YRF's Talent Management department. After watching the trailer of *Nautanki Saala*, Aditya Chopra immediately called me to the mythical fourth floor that very few know exists.

He was shocked by the trailers that were doing the rounds and expressed his surprise to me, despite having advised me to go ahead with Rohan's film since he had been confident about his work. Thankfully, the awards season was on at the time *Nautanki Saala* released and I won the best debut actor award for *Vicky Donor*. My public image as Vicky Donor was so strong, that a few naysayers, no matter how hard they tried, couldn't spell doom for my acting career.

Nautanki Saala was made in the (almost) record time

of forty days, again as a budget constraining exercise. Well-wishers said that I looked jaded in the movie, but they didn't know that we used to shoot continuously for sixteen to eighteen hours every day.

There were times when I felt that things were not going the way they should be. I remember how, during our first script reading session, I got a strong intuition to just run away from the project, but I thought it was just the initial jitters and things would look better after a while. The producers were very confident about the success of the project, though I still felt that something wasn't right.

In all fairness, I don't think the blame rests entirely on Rohan Sippy. Perhaps the makers took *Vicky Donor* as a template to make a small-budget money-spinner. *Nautanki Saala* wasn't a flop; it recovered much more than the budget it was made in, but I don't think it achieved the intended target numbers. I was also disappointed with the kind of feel that was portrayed in the teasers, songs, trailers and promos.

Of course, I had done much more beyond that kiss in the movie! But to keep harping on it and showcasing it repeatedly was a desperate attempt to grab some eyeballs. I expressed my displeasure and, thankfully, it was soon removed from the trailer and the song. Nevertheless, I am happy that this stumble happened at a very early stage in my career.

Code #14: Had I waited for the script of *Nautanki Saala* to be written before signing it, perhaps I could have avoided the misstep it turned out to be. Patience and wisdom is something that even the patient and wise strive for.

10

Life in Cinema Ki Hai Dua

IN MOMENTS OF solitude, I sit and wonder if this is what I had wanted from life. I always knew that I wanted to become an actor in this lifetime. But I didn't imagine in my wildest dreams the 'baraat' and 'baraatis' that would accompany the fulfillment of this ambition. In a big fat Punjabi wedding, there are a few people you really love and respect. There are also many who have to be acknowledged and treated well, just because they are elders and are somehow connected to the family tree. Till this point, there aren't too many worries, and things are under control. The problem begins when the guest list explodes and people who you didn't even know existed are attending your wedding and raiding the bar as if they've paid for the mandap. Now think of the immediate family as my co-stars, directors, technicians and all others involved with the film in any way... They deserve all the love and respect.

The troublemakers are usually those who have nothing to do with me beyond being spectators of my films. The gossip-mongers are the ones who really drive me up the wall. The trailer of *Nautanki Saala* had just about released and was getting varied reactions. Some liked me, some were talking about the kissing scene and, thankfully, many loved the songs—especially 'Saddi gali', composed by Rochak and me, that had started topping the charts.

That was when the Kunal Kohli controversy erupted, and malicious talks about success having gone to my head started doing the rounds. This was just one of the dozen things that were being written and spoken about me at that time. I can't clarify my stand to everybody, but I did what I could. I know it sounds strange coming from me, who once made a living out of talking to and about movie stars, making fun of them and their films, but as the saying goes, karma is a bitch.

The biggest setback of being the interviewee is that you have no control over the questions that will be asked, and no matter what reply you give, the interviewer will go ahead and publish his own version of the statement. This then leads to a series of reactions to the published word, starting from your own staff and going right up to those hobnobbing at Page 3 parties.

While I can still understand speculations about the changing equation between Tahira and me, what really upset me was the rumor of my death. Frankly speaking, it just amused me and gave me a moment of cheap thrill as I had joined the list of celebs who were rumored to be dead while being still alive and kicking. But it also had some unpleasant consequences.

Once the news of my supposed death reached my family back home in Chandigarh, they were obviously shocked and shattered. My grandfather, who is a heart patient, didn't know how to react, but thankfully they called me up immediately and could finally breathe again after they realized I wasn't dead, as some sections of the media would have them believe. Phew!

Getting back to the list of the annoying 'baraatis', one bunch I really dislike are those who want to make a quick buck just off the fact that they know me from somewhere. I wouldn't mind them making money off me, if they were kind enough to share the loot, but alas. While I was shooting for *Bewakoofiyaan* in Delhi, right before I was about to give my shot, my phone rang and I got to know that our male domestic help had committed suicide. That was one scary phase of my life.

To make matters worse, one silly friend called me up to tell me, 'Tu toh yaar sachi star ban gaya!' I was quite bewildered. I thought it would be an empathetic call out of concern. On asking him what he meant, he said, 'Arre yaar, chori-dakaeti toh common logon ke ghar hoten hain, rapes our suicides stars ke ghar!' I was shocked. And I'll leave it at that.

Another crazy one was when I was asked if I was supposed to be in Delhi that evening to promote my upcoming film, *Bewakoofiyaan*, along with my co-star, Sonam Kapoor. The said event was called...hold your breath...HOLI SHIT. It was a dance party to celebrate Holi. Talk about creativity. SHIT. SHIT. SHIT.

But how could we be in Mumbai and Delhi simultaneously? It was too short a notice to even arrange for body doubles. The organizers had publicized the event on social media, and had sold tickets to make shitloads of money. We didn't even know about this development. Enthusiastic fans and followers were looking forward to being a part of a star-studded Holi dance party or whatever it was. Thanks to the ever-efficient PR machinery of YRF, however, immediate damage control was done.

I am not sure if the organizers returned the money to those who had bought the tickets, but yes, these are the lengths that people go to make money.

Thanks to the fortress that YRF afforded me, these scams gradually stopped. There are a few more in the list of annoying 'baraatis', but enough of them. Oh wait, there is one incident I can't not mention. These 'baraatis' made me pay a heavy price once. We were shooting for *Nautanki Saala* at a studio in Kandivili, when we were informed that some ruffians had smashed my car and some vanity vans.

We later got to know a security guard (who was just doing his job) bruised one man's ego by not letting his car pass through. The man, who belonged to a political party, decided to vent out his anger by calling other goons and smashing cars and other expensive things lying in the vicinity. No one had done any wrong, but we ended up paying through our respective noses.

∎

Anyway, that's enough about my sob stories. A watershed moment in my life was when I was offered a three-film deal with YRF. The three letters, 'Y' 'R' 'F', meant the world to me, especially as an actor in Bollywood. One would have to be in acute denial if these three letters didn't inspire awe. Just like every other actor walking the streets of the western suburbs of Mumbai, I too wanted to be associated with the YRF label in any which way.

Even before the release of my second film, my ex-boss at MTV, Ashish Patil, who, as I've mentioned before, is the CEO of Y-films and head of talent management in YRF, offered me a three-film deal with the biggest and the most reputed production house of the country. 'No' isn't even an option when the offer comes from YRF. So, despite not having liked the script that was offered to me all that much, I signed on the dotted line without as much so blinking an eye. Just getting to shake hands with the almost mythical Aditya Chopra was a mean feat in itself, one that I will narrate to my grandkids someday.

Once the initial euphoria of this masterstroke of luck had settled, my world changed. I was not 'Oye Vicky' or 'Ae sperm donor' anymore; at least not in the power corridors of B-town. It was as if I had put on weight. I couldn't feel the weight, but somehow others could see it. Not that I ever threw my weight around, but suddenly I was being taken seriously. I never take myself seriously, though, I swear.

Despite all that was happening, the fact remained that I was still the simpleton from Chandigarh that I always was. I couldn't plan, strategize or do any of those intelligent-sounding things my contemporaries apparently did. I wouldn't kill for a role. At most, I would humbly request the director to allow me to audition for the part.

The best thing to happen to me post signing the deal with YRF is that I don't feel like an outsider anymore. The fraternity feels like family. It's another thing that I still get star-struck when Shahrukh Khan enters the room. Some things just don't change. Having said that, it feels like I am in a very happy and positive space, especially every time I enter the YRF studio. Now it feels like home.

In this cut-throat world of showbiz, the one thing that gives me a high is the music I create with my dear childhood friend and partner-in-crime, Rochak Kohli. We started our journeys almost simultaneously. Years before 'Paani da rang' became a rage thanks to *Vicky Donor*, little did we know how far would we go together in life. It feels like yesterday that we sat together and created the song, back in college.

Together, Rochak and I have composed many songs that we plan to release gradually, maybe in the films that I act in, or perhaps as singles, like my first single 'O Heeriye' and now 'Mitti di khushboo'. Music has been a balancing factor in my life, quite like the way my family keeps me grounded. Making music makes me happy...very happy. The kind of music that we make brings a smile to the listener's face. It makes them feel good about the world around them. I want to continue making music and will always remain an actor/singer.

I am often asked how my collaboration with Rochak works so seamlessly. The question always makes me smile. I think no creative collaboration can work without friction. If there is no friction, perhaps something isn't right there, maybe it is the sign of creative stagnation. We have our fair share of disagreements; it's just that the tabloids don't get to know about it. For us, our music is above everything.

Talking about creative collaboration reminds me of my equation with Shoojit da. Here again, it isn't about box office figures or anything to do with money. Many were surprised to see my name in the end-credits of *Madras Café*, that too as an assistant director. It wasn't as if Shoojit da was falling short of assistants.

I assisted him to satiate my need for understanding cinema from close quarters. I wanted to be in a place where I could just learn without worrying about my hair and makeup.

If Shoojit da doesn't cast me in a film of his, I will never hold it against him—I know that he will cast me *only* if I fit the bill. Not just fit the bill, but fit the bill to the T. You'll understand what I'm saying when you see our next collaboration, *Agra ka Dabra*. I have utmost respect for his craft and will never let go of an opportunity to learn from him, in whatever capacity he allows me to be associated with his projects.

Please don't jump to the conclusion that I harbor any hope of turning director. I don't; at least not as long as people want to watch me act, and definitely not as long as I keep getting good scripts. I am an actor, and would like to hang my boots with the makeup still on my face, and Uday (my spot boy) fussing over me. Well, there's still a long way to go for all that...

Coming back to the present, I wonder if I would want my life to play out the way it did. Is there anything at all that I would like to change if I could? My mind doesn't wait for even a heartbeat to reply—no. I don't want anything to change. It has been an amazing ride, and I have enjoyed every bit of it. Hmm...perhaps I wish Darshan (my driver for the last five years) had better presence of mind. Come on...let's change that right away. (Jokes apart, through, he's a nice guy; just that he's a bit of a scatterbrain.)

Every now and then, people ask me how I manage my life between two cities. My family is in Chandigarh and my work in Mumbai. I love Chandigarh and keep going back at every opportunity I get. Tahira is the balancing factor in my life, the anchor that keeps me grounded. She is the reason I am happy. If you ever spot me smiling like a goofy idiot, I must be thinking about her and the wonderful moments that we have shared.

And the kids! If you look at my son, you would never be able to associate the name 'Virajveer' with his face. If 'happiness' was a human being, it would be him. And, not to forget the latest diva to enter the Khurrana family—my little bundle of joy, Varushka. I feel really blessed every day, touchwood! And I have no qualms in admitting that I am indeed the youngest father in the industry.

Code #15: Of all the codes that one cracks, the emotional code is the most important one. You could be the richest or the most powerful human being in the world, but if you are not at peace with your emotional side, everything else is worthless. I am not even talking about how you feel for your spouse or your partner; even if you are single, and are at peace with your inner demons, you are mostly sorted.

11

Bollywood: Still Uncoding

I HAD JUST stepped out of the special screening of *Bewakoofiyaan* that was held for my peers and friends from the fraternity. There was something amiss that I felt at that moment. I never really wanted to do *Bewakoofiyaan*. I somewhere assumed that the script would eventually evolve from the first draft I had read. *Bewakoofiyaan*, being my first film with YRF, didn't come across as the grand YRF film that I had grown up watching and wanted to be a part of.

I felt very uneasy at that moment. Everybody around was being nice to me, no doubt; they were all praises for my work in the film. I hung around there for a bit, shook hands, faked smiles, and then I just left the place and came back home. My phone kept ringing all the time; there were numerous text messages, but I was numb by this time.

That evening, sitting all by myself, I was cracking the most important code of my life, the most essential self-note too. I learnt that one should always follow one's instincts. No other factor should influence your decisions other than your conviction in the script. The script is the king in our line of work. I remember being awestruck on meeting Rohan Sippy in the same office where the epic *Sholay* was narrated. But these things shouldn't be the reason for taking on a project.

Thankfully, nothing affects me too much beyond a point. I get neither very ecstatic about anything nor completely down and out. I like to think of myself as a goofy sufi. As they say, there is light at the end of the tunnel; I found my light in the dead of that night. *Bewakoofiyaan* released to a lukewarm response, and thankfully the critics liked my acting in it. But none of it mattered to me. It felt like I had snapped out of the film for good.

I have learned a lot from my failures, and I am sure I wouldn't have been half as sorted if I hadn't. As the lines from Emily Dickinson's poem *Success is Counted Sweetest* say:

Success is counted sweetest
By those who ne'er succeed.
To comprehend a nectar
Requires sorest need.

The truth is that a majority of the films here are made just because a star-pair's dates are available. Some films are made because the producer and his wife want to holiday abroad. The reasons why films get made are as random and bizarre as that. Passionate filmmakers like Shoojit da are an exception to the rule.

Was I taking movies too seriously? Hell, yeah! Compared to Adi or Shoojit da, my knowledge of cinema is smaller than SRK's cameo in *Luck By Chance*. Then why was I trying to intellectualize the debacle of a film that didn't even promise to change the world? Breathe in. Breathe out. Is the light at the end of the tunnel still visible? It is.

The truth is, no matter how hard I try, I can't take cinema lightly; be it *Bewakoofiyaan* or any of my forthcoming films. It's your choices that make or break you. If I have put in a hard day's work in something, I will take it seriously. Good cinema brings out the happy child inside me. I will do everything it takes to make my film a better one. No, I will not teach the director how to shoot a scene. I will just hope that my enthusiasm rubs off on everyone involved in making the film.

I'm not trying to say that I will only act in films that promise to change the world. I know it's too long a shot for a regular Hindi film to try and change even a single person. My only attempt will be to make sure that whatever film I choose to do will deliver on its promises. The case in point here is *Hawaaizaada*, the film that is all set to release. It is a biopic, and is true to its genre. Make no mistake, I am not saying that *Hawaaizaada* will be the best biopic to come out of our industry. I am just saying that I believed in the script and therein lies an essential step in cracking the code.

Just a few weeks ago, I was made to hear a narration of a script for a sex comedy. As much as it made me cringe and squirm in my seat, I couldn't be rude to those who had come to narrate the film to me. I laughed where they were expecting me to laugh; I pretended to be shocked on cue. In that narration I was at my acting best. Oscar level stuff...hah!

Needless to say, I jovially declined the film saying that the material was too risqué for an actor like me to pull off, without making a sorry joke out of myself. I hope whoever eventually does choose to act in that film does justice to the role offered, and it goes on to become the one of the best sex comedies ever made. No kidding. As long as they leave me out of it, I'm fine.

Every film that is written usually finds its own bunch of takers. Sometimes the script catches an actor's fancy; at times, a producer sees moneymaking potential in it... Every script finds a taker; unless it's a really jinxed project. The only difference is that the bunch of people who come together to make it happen will vary from script to script or star to star.

For instance, if the bound script of *Vicky Donor* was given to five different filmmakers, they would make their own versions of it, depending on their individual sensibilities. Suppose Karan Johar liked the script of *Vicky Donor* and took it to SRK, it could become a 'My Name is Vicky Donor' sort of game-changer. The same script when given to, say, Anurag Kashyap, might look totally different...a neo-noir version maybe?

(*Disclaimer: I would love to work with everybody who makes good films—commercial or otherwise.*)

What I'm trying to say here is that we all can coexist peacefully. There is no dearth of work for anybody. If you have a Twitter account and follow even a dozen B-towners, you will see what I mean. Hrithik Roshan is all praise for Priyanka Chopra's *Mary Kom*, Ranveer Singh is happily going gaga over Deepika Padukone's *Finding Fanny*, and so on and so forth. This scenario couldn't have even been imagined a decade or so ago.

All the actors seem to have signed up for the so-called 'mutual admiration society'. This is another pointer in cracking the code: It makes sense to coexist without stepping on anybody's toes. There is only so much that we all can do in one lifetime. We can hope and pray that the best offers come to us, but that's about it. Who gets what or how much is beyond our control.

This growing camaraderie amongst actors is a big lesson for everybody. Despite being insecure, narcissistic, vain and generally competitive, the recent crop of actors seems to be comfortable with the films that land up in their kitty. No matter how much anybody tries, there is only so much one can do. I really admire the way Priyanka balances a multi-starrer like *Dil Dhadakne Do* with a gritty *Mary Kom*. Just the way Ranbir Kapoor does a *Barfi* and *Yeh Jawaani Hai Deewani*.

Of course, there are exceptions like superstars, Shahrukh and Salman Khan, who have attained the Midas touch. Whatever they lay their hands on turns into cinema gold. Critics may pull their hair out, saying that these superstars play to the gallery and don't experiment, but nothing succeeds like success. Let's save this for another book, shall we?

The bottom line is that success begets success and happiness begets happiness. There is no point holding a grudge over your peers' success. Why not focus on how you could better your craft? Why not focus on making better career choices? As of this day, it has become a big, level playing field. We all are just as good or bad as our last outing, in the movies or in real life. The point is to be positive and optimistic. If you can be even half as energetic as Ranveer Singh, you are right on the right track!

As I was saying, the 'meta' code is to know your best and your worst qualities, and then making peace with them. If I had the sensibility or insensibility to pull off a raunchy film, I would have jumped at the offer. But what If I was offered a superhero film; how far would I go? Could I pull off a *Krrish*? Would I be able to beef up like Hrithik and pull out all the stops? I would. I will. Will I be seen in a sex comedy? No, I wouldn't even be seen dead in a sex comedy.

That's all it takes to crack the code—being comfortable in your skin, amidst your good and bad. The magical moment of truth will decide your journey. It's difficult to crack, but not impossible. I don't mean to say that I have completely cracked this code, but I am on my way there. Will I become a superstar? I don't know. Will I be a happy and content man? I really think so.

A secret to cracking the code is to make your own codes. One man's medicine is another man's poison. At a holistic level, the code remains the same—be truthful to yourself. You can lie to the entire world, but at the end of the day, it is just you and the person in the mirror. It is just your eyes staring at the roof, gaping at a vast nothingness, moments before you fall asleep. If you ensure or even try to ensure that in that dark moment you can see the light at the end of the tunnel, you have cracked the code. Congratulations.

Perhaps after a decade or so, we could exchange notes on how this entire 'cracking the code' worked for us. Did I crack it? Did I help you crack the code? Maybe I should rewrite these codes when life has taught me more lessons. But shouldn't I have shared my secret with you at the soonest? That's the least I could do, for all the goodness that the universe has bestowed upon me.

The one thing I have learnt is that it isn't about

how much you take; it's about how much you give back. I guess that's all I have for you in this book.

See you at the movies!

Ayushmann bhava.

Acknowledgements

I am eternally thankful for all my experiences, some good some bad, that led me to writing this book. Since experiences can't be devoid of people, I am also grateful to all those who loved me, hated me, had faith in me, pulled me down, appreciated my art, cursed me, envied me, loathed me and helped me. I am glad that all these people, many of whom are mentioned in the book, came into my life. It has led me to be what I am. And I am at peace with myself.

Amongst all these, there are a few people who are permanent fixtures in my life—those who will be with me always and unconditionally. I will always be indebted to my father, P. Khurrana; my mother, Poonam; my wife, Tahira; and my brother, Aparshakti. Apart from my family members, I would like to mention my manager, Rani Mol, for her rock solid support and her husband, Kiran Prakash Rao, for proofreading this with a lot of passion.

Finally, I would like to acknowledge the power that exists within you and me—the power that will take us ahead, and help us reach our full potential.